The Runaways

A New and Original Story

Nat Gould

The Runaways: A New and Original Story

Copyright © 2021 Bibliotech Press
All rights reserved

ISBN: 978-1-63637-498-7

CONTENTS

NAT GOULD: AN APPRECIATION

NAT GOULD'S novels of the Turf are read and enjoyed by multitudes of men and women all over the world. That in itself is a guarantee of literary merit. Had he been a stylist, the sale of his hundred odd books would never have run into a score of millions. He wrote to please and not to puzzle, to give pleasure and not to educate, and his reward came in the gratitude of a host of admirers of clean, healthy fiction.

His main theme was the King of Sports and the Sport of Kings. Nat Gould dearly loved a horse, and so does the great British public, including those who have no liking for racing. It is a characteristic as national as our admiration of ships, sailors and the sea. The theme fascinated him, and, combined with a gift for writing, was one of the secrets of his success. Another reason for his almost boundless popularity is to be found in the "atmosphere" of his stories, which is created without elaborate literary setting. The machinery of it is hidden by reason of its very artlessness. The romance is told in a plain, straightforward way that carries intense conviction, and though the plots are neither subtle nor involved, they are unfolded in so vigorous and lifelike a manner that few people who pick up one of Nat Gould's novels are able to put it down before having finished the last chapter. Few modern writers can boast that they are read and understood at a single sitting.

His novels ring true. They are clean, manly and sincere. There is nothing vicious about them. As The Times truly said of Nat Gould in its obituary notice of him, "He must have written some millions of words, but few of them were wasted, if a rattling good story makes a reader happier and more contented for having read it."

Such praise is praise indeed, for literature that is involved and appeals to a select few obviously cannot have the influence of literature that embraces so large a section of the population. To have added to the enjoyment of so vast a number of young and old, rich and poor, were a monument worthy of any man.

Nathaniel Gould was born in Manchester in 1857, and died in 1919. His wide experience as a journalist in England and Australia doubtless explained his methods of rapid workmanship, while his travels in the Antipodes and elsewhere afforded him that "local colour" which is not the least pleasing characteristic of his novels. He not only wrote of outdoor life, but enjoyed it, for racing, driving and gardening were his hobbies.

E. LATON BLACKLANDS

CHAPTER I

AS THE SNOW FALLS

Redmond Maynard stood at the dining-room window gazing at the deep-dyed reflection upon the snow of the blood-red setting sun. The leafless trees, with their gnarled trunks and gaunt, twisted branches, spreading fiercely in imprecation at the hardness of their lot, resembled giant monsters from an unknown world. These diseased protruding growths put on all manner of fantastic shapes, as his eyes dwelt first upon one, then upon another. It was the shortening winter's day drawing near a close, and a spirit of melancholy brooded over the landscape. On such an evening as this, the thoughts of thinking men are apt to draw comparisons which bring vividly before them the uncertainty of life, and the prospects of that something after death which has never been understood, never will be, until each one solves the problem by going out into the eternal night.

It seemed to Redmond Maynard that he was peering into a mystery he had no hope of solving. He was not a godless man, neither was he a man whose life had been altogether well spent. His mistakes had been many; he acknowledged this, and thereby robbed his detractors of selfish victories. Slowly the sun sank, and as it dipped lower and lower into obscurity the red shadows on the snow grew fainter, the harshness melted, and a gentle warmth seemed to mingle with the biting cold. The glow remained some time after the sun had disappeared, and Redmond Maynard stood in the same position watching it.

Then, almost without warning—

> "Out of the bosom of the air,
> Out of the cloud folds of her garment shaken—
> Over the woodlands brown and bare,
> Over the harvest fields forsaken,
> Silent and soft and slow,
> Descended the snow."

It came fluttering down from the "bosom of the air," to nestle in the bosom of the earth, to mingle with the white mantle lying there, to lie pure and undefiled until an angry thaw turned all its beauty into dulness and decay. How gently the flakes fell, and Redmond Maynard watched them with the warm glow from the fire shedding flickering light behind and around him.

"Shall I draw the curtain, sir?"

"No."

The man silently left the room, sighing as he did so, thinking to himself, "It's two years come to-night since Mr. Ulick left home. I wonder will he come back. The Squire's thinking of it now. God help 'em both."

"There will be no darkness to-night," muttered Redmond Maynard, as he saw a silvery ray cross the lawn in front of the house. No darkness, perhaps not, but in his heart there was a desolate feeling deeper than the blackness of night. Two years ago Ulick Maynard walked out of that very room, and had not since returned. Bitter words were spoken between father and son. Both were proud. The accusation fell upon Ulick like a thunderbolt; for the moment he was stunned. Then, with his frozen blood bursting into a fiery torrent, he hurled back the insult his father had put upon him. He stayed not to think what causes led Redmond Maynard to make the charge. In his mind no evidence, however conclusively circumstantial, ought to have been considered sufficient to make his father speak such words.

The elder man recoiled under the shock. Given an opportunity, he would have recalled his words. But the chance was not allowed.

"Believing, as you must, or you would not have accused me, that I am guilty of this infamy, I will no longer inflict my presence upon you, sir. Good-night."

No more, no less; those were the very words, and Ulick Maynard left the room. That was two years ago, and nothing had been heard of him since.

"Ulick!" called his father, as the door closed behind him. "Come back at once. Ulick!"

No answer was returned, and the still angry man thought, "He'll get over it by morning. Gad, what a devil of a temper he has. He's the culprit, safe enough, although Eli will not hear of it."

Ulick Maynard did not "get over it by morning." He disappeared, and his father had never been the same man since. Without drawing the curtains, Redmond Maynard left the window, and, walking to the fireplace, stood with his back to the blaze.

Stretched on the hearthrug was a strong, powerful, shaggy wolf-hound. Bersak raised his long, lean head, and looked at his master, but observing no sign that his services were required, stretched himself out again at full length with a sigh of satisfaction. There was ample room between the dog and the hearth for his master to stand, and Redmond Maynard looked down upon him from a height of nearly six feet.

"His dog," he muttered. "Bersak, where's Ulick?"

The hound sprang to his feet and stood alert, every nerve strained, head erect, listening for footsteps he had not heard for two years, but which he would have recognised even amidst the deadening snow. Man and dog looked at each other. That question had been asked before.

"Bersak, where's Ulick?"

Rather shaky the tones this time, and something in them affected the hound, for he lifted up his head and whined; the sound would have developed into a howl, but Redmond Maynard placed his hand on his head and said—

"Don't howl, Bersak, I could not stand it. Lie down. Good dog, lie down."

Obedient to the word of command, Bersak lowered himself— no other word adequately expresses the dog's movement,—to the hearthrug, and with his fore-paws stretched out watched the Squire's face.

How much would Redmond Maynard have given to see the door open and his son Ulick walk in. All he possessed—aye, more, many years of his life. He knew how Bersak would have leapt [to] his feet with a mighty bark of welcome, and a spring forward until his strong paws reached Ulick's shoulders.

3

He fixed his eyes on the door, and as he did so it opened. But it was not Ulick entering, although the newcomer brought a faint smile on his face.

"Irene!" he exclaimed, as the vision in furs came across the fire-lit room; "this is good of you. However did you get here; is it still snowing?"

"No, Squire, it is not snowing, although there is plenty of snow; and as to how I came here, well—look at my boots," and she held up her dress and disclosed a pair of strong "lace-ups," fitting perfectly her well-shaped feet.

"So you walked all the way from the Manor, and with the express object of cheering a lonely old man on a depressing winter's evening. I call that good of you, positively charitable, but Irene Courtly's name is ever associated with good works," said the Squire.

"I am afraid the good work on this occasion is closely allied with selfishness," she replied, smiling. "Being alone, I appreciate the feelings of others similarly situated, and that is how I came to think of you."

"Alone!" he exclaimed. "Where is Warren?"

"Gone to London. Important business. No hunting, you see, Squire," she said, with a laugh he thought had not a very true ring about it.

Redmond Maynard gave an impatient gesture, and Bersak pushed his head against her hand in doggish sympathy. Irene Courtly noticed the movement, and said—

"He really had to go; he assured me it was absolutely necessary," she said.

Warren Courtly had also added. "I'll be back in a few days, Irene. Run over and see the Squire, you will be company for each other."

"You cannot humbug me, Irene," said Redmond Maynard. "He's tired of the country because there is no sport, and I call it downright selfish of him to go up to town and leave you behind at Anselm Manor."

"But, really, I did not wish to go, Squire."

4

"You mean it?"

"Yes, most decidedly."

"Then pull off those furs; let me send Bob over for your things and your maid, and stay here until Warren returns," said the Squire.

This time the laugh was hearty enough, and she said—

"Impetuous as ever, Squire. I only wish I could."

"And what is to prevent your doing so?"

"My duty towards my neighbours," said Irene, laughing.

"Love your neighbour as yourself, and I am your nearest neighbour," he answered.

Then, going to the window, he opened it, and, putting out his arm for a few moments, drew it in again and showed her the snowflakes on his coat-sleeve.

"You cannot possibly return to the Manor in such weather," he said, and touched the bell.

"Can you drive, or ride, to Anselm Manor, Bob?" he asked.

The man shook his head doubtfully.

"I'll try, sir."

"Take the old mare and 'the tub,' and bring Mrs. Courtly's maid back. She will know what her mistress requires."

"Yes, sir, I'll manage it," replied Bob Heather, with alacrity.

Mary Marley, Mrs. Courtly's maid, was Bob Heather's favourite, and he had an idea she preferred him to any of her admirers.

"The maid did it," said the Squire, with a smile. "I doubt if he would have undertaken the journey for the luggage alone."

Irene laughed, and then, in a serious mood, said, as she stroked Bersak's head, "Do you think it right for me to remain here. You are my oldest friend, and my guardian until I married Warren. Ought I to stay?"

5

"Of course, of course," he replied impatiently. "It is snowing fast again. Warren would not expect you to go home on such a night."

She settled down to spend a quiet evening with him. She knew what this night meant to him, what it might have meant to her had all gone well with Ulick.

Watching him as he sat with the firelight on his face, she noticed how he had aged during the past year. No, not aged exactly, for he was still a firm, strong, active man; but there was something in his noble, if severe, face that told of a great struggle racking him within.

She knew the largeness of his heart, and his notions of honour, which many modern hypocrites laughed at, because their little minds could not grasp his greatness. She remembered how he guarded her [as] his own child when her father, Colonel Carstone, died and left her as a legacy to his old friend. He brought her as a girl of sixteen to Hazelwell, and said—

"Irene, this is your home. Your father gave you to me, and it is a sacred gift. You will get on with Ulick, he is a good lad, and you have known each other for some years. Hazelwell will be the brighter for your presence."

She revered Redmond Maynard above all men, and whatever he did she considered right, until—until Ulick left his home.

"He is thinking of him now," she thought. "Oh, why does he not come home? The old scandal is dead; I have forgiven him, surely he has—he must."

Bersak sat with his head in her lap looking into her face, his sharp, keen eyes blinking, and occasionally he turned to look at the silent figure in the chair. Irene did not disturb him, but to know his thoughts she would have given much.

She saw his hands clench the chair tightly—sure sign of a strong man's emotion.

Quietly she rose from her seat, took a footstool, placed it beside him, and sat at his feet. She laid her head on his knee; Bersak followed her and lay at her feet. They formed a pretty group in the firelight's glow. The room was warm and cosy, although large;

6

outside, the snow was still falling, adding steadily to the frozen mass upon which it descended.

Redmond Maynard placed his hand on her head and gently stroked her hair. She remained silent and quite still.

"It is like old times to have you here again," he said at length.

"And I am very glad to be with you. Will you play chess, shall I read to you, or will you talk?" she said.

"Being a woman, Irene, I will talk to you."

"Am I such a chatterbox?" she answered, laughing.

"Not that, anything but that. You speak when you have something to say; you are not an aimless chatterer."

"Warren says my tongue is never still."

"Warren is an ass," he snapped.

"Oh, dear no, not at all. He is by no means stupid."

"I retract; I ought not to have made use of the expression."

"I will keep it to myself in strict confidence," she replied, with a smile.

The door opened, and a maid said—

"Shall I light the lamps, sir?"

"Please."

The room was soon aglow with a soft, delicate light, and as the maid went out she said to herself—

"Well, I never. The ways of these gentry are past me. Fancy her sitting like that, and going to stop here all night. It's not respectable."

She was a new maid, with a narrow mind and a relaxable conscience, which could be stretched to any required length to suit her own purposes.

The maid, the luggage, and Bob Heather duly arrived. Bob

had taken good care Mary Marley should not be cold during the drive.

"Are you tired, Irene?"

"No. I will sit up until you are ready to go."

"An hour longer, and then I shall pack you off," he said.

"And you?"

"I shall be up all night."

"All night?" she exclaimed, in surprise, "Why?"

"Because it is the night, two years ago, that Ulick left home. I sat up all night on this date last year. I know it will be on a night such as this he will come back."

"To-night, not to-night? Will he come home to-night?" she asked, eagerly.

"How can I tell, child? If he does not I must wait another year," he said, sadly.

"You have forgiven him?"

"Yes; but not his sin," he said.

"Are you sure, quite sure, it is his sin?" she asked.

"Unfortunately, there is no doubt about it."

"But Eli Todd——" she commenced.

"Is wrong," he answered. "He is blinded by his faith in Ulick. Eli would sacrifice even more than he has done for him, and God knows how he has suffered."

"I wish we had Eli's faith," she replied.

CHAPTER II

THE RUNAWAYS

There was a stud of thoroughbreds at Hazelwell, not large, but select, some of the mares boasting of blue blood such as can seldom be obtained after much search. Eli Todd was the manager of the stud, and lived in a small but picturesque and comfortable cottage on the estate. He served in the —th Hussars with Colonel Carstone, and during the time they were in India he acquired a considerable knowledge of horses of every description. He handled the Colonel's "Walers," and broke them in cleverly; he also trained the Colonel's horses for the races, and on one occasion had the audacity to declare he meant to win the Viceroy's Cup for his master, a feat he all but accomplished, as the Scout ran a good second for that coveted trophy.

When Colonel Carstone died, and Irene was committed to the care of Redmond Maynard, Eli Todd entered his service at the same time. It was owing to Irene that he did so. She persuaded her guardian that Eli was a veritable wonder in the management of horses, and that she was perfectly certain that if his services were secured Hazelwell Stud would benefit thereby.

Ulick Maynard backed up her recommendation, declaring he had cast curious eyes upon Eli ever since he returned from India with the Colonel.

"Lose no time in securing him," said Ulick; "such a man will be snapped up at once. Don't lose him whatever you do."

Redmond Maynard engaged Eli to manage his stud, and also to superintend the hunters and all the horses on the estate—a step he had never regretted. Eli was a widower with one child, a daughter, Janet Todd. She was about the same age as Irene, and a bright, merry, mischievous, exceedingly pretty girl. Vanity was her besetting sin, but apart from this she was of an amiable disposition, and innocent of any desire beyond harmless flirtations. Naturally her father idolised her, and it was mainly on her account he accepted the position Mr. Maynard offered him.

The night that Redmond Maynard sat up, hoping against hope that his son would return, Eli Todd was in a troubled state of mind.

Like his master, he dated the great misfortune of his life two years back from that night. He recalled vividly how his daughter Janet had kissed him good-night and then gone to bed. Her manner gave no indication of what was to befall during the next few hours.

He remembered how he sat waiting for her to come down to breakfast, wondering what kept her so long. Her room was above that in which he sat, and he heard no movement on the floor above. The strain became too great, and at last he could bear it no longer. He did not ring for the housekeeper, but crept upstairs and tapped gently at her door. There was no answer, and as he sat now, two years after, he felt again the throbbing of his heart in anticipation of some unknown evil he experienced on that occasion. He knocked again, and then slowly, noiselessly opened the door.

The room was empty, the bed had not been slept upon. Dazed and bewildered, he failed at first to understand what it meant. The stillness stunned him, and he groped his way forward like a blind man. Mechanically he ran his hands over the spotless counterpane, seeking, feeling for that he knew he should not find. He looked under the bed, in a closet, and even in her wardrobe; she was hiding, playing him a trick, but where had she hidden herself?

He sat down in the chair at her bedside and looked helplessly about the room. He fingered the candlestick which stood on a small table near the bed, examining it with unusual interest. There was an old pair of snuffers there, and he took them up and pressed the wick, which stuck fast, and the candle with the snuffers attached fell on the table. He put the empty candlestick on the bed and got up.

Walking to the window, he drew up the blinds and looked round the room again. He was near the dressing-table, and picked up one article after another. He did not look for a letter, a brief note; he would not have found one had he done so. She had gone, left him desolate without one parting word.

Still in a dazed condition, and not fully realising his loss, he went out of the room, closing the door after him, and stumbled downstairs.

Mrs. Marley, his housekeeper, heard him, and came into the room,

"Is Janet ill?" she asked, in a tone of concern.

"Yes," he replied, in a hollow voice. "I will take her breakfast upstairs."

"I can take it myself," she replied.

"No; please let me do it."

"Very well, but you spoil her, Mr. Todd; it is not good for her," said Mrs. Marley.

He laughed strangely, and she looked at him in surprise. He took the tray upstairs, placed it on the table at the bedside, and locked the door as he came out, putting the key in his pocket. Why he did this he failed to understand, except that he wanted time to think.

He was going over again everything that happened that terrible night. He had considered it many times, and he would not lay the guilt at Ulick's door; no, not even after two years of grave suspicion, which had not yet been removed. He once more saw the door open and Ulick Maynard come in out of the snowy night. He heard the startled cry Janet gave as she sprang from her chair, and her exclamation, "Mr. Ulick, what are you doing here?" rang in his ears.

"Eli, I want to sit down and think," Ulick had said, and, wonderingly, he bade him make the house his home, as he had always done.

Janet, pale and bewildered, left the room.

"Is anything the matter, Mr. Ulick?" asked Eli.

"You'll learn soon enough," was the vague reply; and then he saw Ulick take out his pocket-book and count some notes.

"Have some supper?" said Eli.

"No, I dined at home an hour ago." Then he looked hard at Eli. Surely he knew what people were saying, knew of the gossip about Janet. It amazed him when he had to acknowledge that Eli

Todd was the only person in the village who was in ignorance of what concerned him most.

"Where's Janet? I must speak to her," said Ulick.

Eli called her, and she came slowly into the room, her face as pale as death.

"Mr. Ulick wishes to speak to you. I'll leave you together, I want to look at Blossom again."

What passed between them he never knew; what he did know was that next morning Janet was gone.

As he sat crushed and stunned under the blow, there came a furious knocking at the door, and Mrs. Marley called out in an agitated voice—

"It's the Squire, and isn't he in a rage!"

As Eli sat in his chair by the fire he again conjured up the picture of Redmond Maynard striding furiously into the room, knocking the snow from his boots with his hunting crop.

"Is my son here, or has he been here?" he asked, angrily.

"He was here last night," said Eli, in a hollow voice.

"And is he here still?"

"No."

"Where is he?"

"I don't know; he went away after—after——"

"After what?" thundered the Squire.

"After he had seen Janet about something he wished to say to her," said Eli, slowly.

"And where is the hussey; d——n it, man, where is she?"

Eli strode up to him, and looking him full in the face, said—

"Not that word from you, Squire, take it back, take it back; she is my child."

12

Redmond Maynard controlled his feelings.

"It is a hard word, Eli, I ought not to have used it. You have sufficient to bear without that," he said.

"He knows," thought Eli. "How does he know?" and he looked at the Squire, who could not fail to notice his surprise.

"May I speak with your daughter?" said the Squire; and from this Eli knew there was some mystery he did not yet grasp.

"She is gone," he replied, in a low voice, for the first time acknowledging the dreadful truth.

"Left your house!" exclaimed Redmond Maynard.

"Yes. I found her room empty this morning, but I have, so far, concealed her flight from my housekeeper."

Redmond Maynard strode up and down the room, muttering threats and imprecations.

"He has stolen her from you, Eli; but he shall pay for it dearly. He is even a greater scoundrel than I accused him of being," said the Squire.

"Do you know who has tempted my daughter to leave me?" asked Eli, placing his hand on the Squire's arm in his earnestness.

"Man, you must know," replied the Squire, amazed at his stupidity. "Have you noticed nothing wrong with her during the past few weeks?"

"No, my Janet has always been the same to me until last night."

The Squire's rage against Ulick passed all bounds. He had accused him of trifling with Janet's affections, and now, to crown his offence, the graceless fellow had induced her to run away with him.

"My son came here last night," he said. "You left him alone with your daughter, and it was no doubt during that time they planned to go away together. He has taken her from you, Eli, and I hope he will make her an honest woman. To think a son of mine

13

should be such a scoundrel. Ulick, whom I have loved beyond all others, it is too terrible."

At last Eli Todd understood. His daughter, the pride of his life, the prettiest of all the village lasses, was a light o' love, and Ulick, his favourite, to whom he would have entrusted her life, was accused of betraying her. The shock of this discovery overwhelmed him, but he had more faith in Ulick than his father had.

"If a man has tempted my daughter to leave my home and follow him, it is not Mr. Ulick, Squire," said Eli, solemnly. "He'd never do it; he'd cut off his right hand first. You wrong him, and you'll regret the day you taxed him with such a charge."

Redmond Maynard wondered at the man's faith in his son. To his mind the proof was clear as day, especially now Janet Todd had disappeared at the same time as Ulick.

"Your feelings do you credit," he replied; "but the evidence is too clear. You know as well as I that when people hear Ulick and Janet have disappeared, they will say they went together. Can it be otherwise? They have been great friends, constantly meeting, and have often been seen alone together. My son has done you a great and grievous wrong, and I must do all in my power to lessen the blow."

"I'll hear no words against Mr. Ulick, Squire. True, he came here last night, but he left long before Janet could have gone. I will never believe it of him. It was not his nature to do evil. He'll prove it some day. As for my poor lass, God help her. She'll come back to me some day, when her heart is sore and aching for her father's love. Whatever she is, whatever she may have done, I will never refuse her the shelter of my home and name. We don't know all, Squire; there may be something we cannot understand, but which will be explained in the future. But Mr. Ulick! Why, Squire, I'd as soon accuse myself of crime as him."

Two years ago this scene took place between master and man, and Eli still held firm in his belief in the stainless honour of Ulick Maynard. No word had come from Janet during all that time. Where she was he knew not, but he thought of her day and night, and as he went about his work he offered up many a plea for her return.

"The Squire 'll be thinking of Ulick to-night," he muttered, as

14

he rose from his chair, went to the door, and looked out into the night.

Snow was still falling softly, and the moon bathed the landscape in silvery splendour. As he looked, he heard the faint, dull sound of a horse's hoofs on the snow, and the rumble of clogged wheels.

"Where can they be going from the house to-night?" he thought, and then recognised Bob Heather, seated in "the tub," and almost smothered in wraps.

"Hallo, Eli, that you? A nice job I've got, fetching Mrs. Courtly's maid, and a heap of luggage, from Anselm a night like this."

"Going to Anselm!" exclaimed Eli. "What's up there?"

"Seems to me everything's up. Mr. Courtly's gone up to London on most important business, and left Mrs. Courtly alone. He's always got business in London. I'd know what it was if I was her. She came over to see the Squire, and he's made her stop with him. I say, Eli, don't you think she'd have been a lot better off if she'd married Mr. Ulick?"

"Mind your own business," growled Eli. "It don't concern you; and as to what I think, I'll keep it to myself."

"It's two years since he left us, and the Squire's been thinking about it all night. He's got a notion Mr. Ulick will come back at this time of year."

"So he will, and I hope my lass will come too," said Eli.

"You still think they did not go away together?" asked Bob.

"I don't say that, but I'll swear Mr. Ulick never harmed a hair of her head," said Eli.

"He's a rum 'un," thought Bob. "Why, everybody knows they ran off together; that's what made the Squire so bitter."

"Have a glass of ale?" said Eli.

"Thanks, you keep a better tap than they have at Hazelwell."

"I drink it myself," said Eli, smiling, "and order it myself. I expect it's not the Squire's fault if you don't get the best."

"No, it's not. Old Josh knows how many beans make five, and I'll bet he charges top price for the stuff he gets in for us," said Bob.

Eli went indoors and came out with a foaming tankard of ale, which Bob Heather made short work of.

"That will keep me warm," he said, with a sigh of satisfaction.

"You have plenty of rugs, are you afraid the luggage will catch cold?" said Eli, slyly.

"Luggage be blowed," said Bob. "These things are for Mary; she'd never forgive me if she caught a cold," and he shook the reins and proceeded on his journey.

CHAPTER III

RANDOM

Squire Maynard remained in the dining-room throughout the night. Towards morning he fell asleep in his arm-chair, Bersak watching on the rug at his feet. It would have gone ill with the man who attempted to touch the Squire with Bersak on guard. More than one poacher had felt the hound's teeth in his calf, and howled for mercy, and been forgiven on account of the punishment received.

Bersak once saved Ulick's life, or if not his life, at any rate rescued him from being maimed.

A three-year-old bull attacked him, and there was no chance of escape. The furious beast had Ulick at his feet, and was bellowing over him, as a preliminary to goring him, when Bersak came to the rescue. The wolf-hound tore across the field in a direct line for the bull, who, seeing him, raised his head and bellowed forth defiance. On came Bersak, and flew straight at the bull's throat. He tore him terribly, but the animal could not rid himself of his fierce enemy. Never had bull such a mauling, and when Ulick came to himself he saw the dog still dragging his enemy down. It was a long struggle, but Bersak won, and the bull was shot to end his misery.

Bersak's fame spread far and wide, and he had the honour of having several attempts made upon his life by the bad characters in the district.

So, while his master slept, Bersak kept watch; and when the door was opened by Bob Heather in the morning a faint growl warned the intruder that his master still slept. He closed the door and went quietly away, thinking it was a blessing the Squire had not kept awake all night.

A faint light stole into the room as Redmond Maynard awoke, and at first he looked round, hardly realising where he was. Then, as he thought over the events of the previous day, he said to himself, "Not this year. I must be patient; perhaps it will be in the next."

17

Then he drew aside the curtains and looked again upon the wintry scene. A good deal of snow had fallen during the night, and the wind drifted it against the hedges and the trunks of the huge oak trees. There was no sign of life until a hare ran across the lawn into the garden, where there was a plentiful supply of winter vegetables. Presently stealing along with his tail out, head down, and glancing from side to side with a cunning look, came a fox. He, too, crossed the lawn in the track of the hare, and the Squire smiled as he watched him.

"You are having a rest, my friend," he said; "but I think you would prefer the hounds at your heels, and an open country before you, in preference to all the snow. No hunting for weeks, that is what it looks like. Deuce take Warren, I wonder why he always goes to town when there is an excuse handy. Was I right in advising Irene to marry him. I think so, I hope so; but yet I doubt. He is good-looking, has money, a fine estate adjoining mine, bears a good character, as young men go, and yet there is something wanting about him. He must love Irene, no one could help it, but he has no business to leave her alone to her own devices. She is young, has no children yet, nothing to occupy her mind; no, it is not fair to her. In a hunting country like this the free-and-easy intercourse at the meets sometimes leads to danger. Nothing is meant at first, but gradually acquaintance ripens into intimacy, and one cannot well decline to put up a fellow sportsman, even if one's husband be absent. Irene is to be trusted, I know, but she is remarkably handsome, and her good nature is apt to carry her too far in her efforts to please. If only Ulick had—but there, he didn't, so what is the use of thinking about it. Stupid fellow, not to see his way clear, and then to disgrace our name beyond all redemption. I wonder where he is, and where she is?" He stopped soliloquising, and went to the bath-room, from whence, in about half-an-hour, he emerged refreshed and in a more amiable frame of mind. In the breakfast-room he found Irene.

She came forward smiling, and kissed him.

"There, was not that nice? You do not deserve it though, for you sat up all night."

"Who has been telling tales?" he asked.

"Bersak."

18

He laughed as be said, "And, pray, how is Bersak to be held responsible?"

"He took me into the dining-room, and I followed him to your chair. He stood looking at it so comically that I had to laugh. He said as plainly as though he had spoken, 'That's where he sat all night, and I watched him. No fear of anyone touching him with me on guard.'"

"Wonderful," laughed the Squire. "Irene, with Bersak as your instructor and guide, you would quickly find out all my secrets."

"I did not know you had any."

"They are not very terrible, but I possess a few; I must be in the fashion," he said.

"I have no secrets from Warren. I tell him everything."

"I wonder if he tells you everything," thought Redmond Maynard, and said aloud, "That's right, my dear, never have any secrets from your husband."

She poured out his coffee for him, and handed it herself. She tempted him with a dainty portion of pigeon pie, and then insisted upon some anchovy paste.

"I'll tell you what it is, Irene; I have not made such a good breakfast for many a day. Your presence is appetising."

She was pleased to hear him talk in this strain, more like his old self. Somehow, she did not miss Warren; she hardly gave him a thought. As for Anselm Manor, she much preferred Hazelwell, as it was more like home.

At the Manor she often felt nervous and depressed when alone, peopling the old place with the figures of clean-shaven monks in long brown gowns, pacing up and down the corridors, Bible in hand or telling their beads, and thinking of things earthly while engaged spiritually.

Anselm Manor, in the centuries gone by, had been a monastery, and it was an ancestor of Warren Courtly who founded it. Harry the Eighth upset many monkish arrangements, but, strange to say, he allowed Anselm to exist. The much-married monarch never even visited the place on a monk hunt, although it contained much valuable plate, and the eighth Henry had a penchant for other people's property.

In Anselm Manor Irene had come across an old deed, or she fancied it a deed. It looked dirty and musty, and smelt abominably enough to be such a document, which, after much labour in deciphering, she found was a gift in perpetuity from Henry the Eighth, by the Grace of God, to one Anselm Courtly, of the monastery and all the lands belonging to it.

She thought it highly probable that the King had secured the said Anselm's good offices, at a price, when some of his numerous matrimonial troubles arose.

Irene thought the Manor a fine old place, but she preferred to see its rooms filled with scarlet coats to imaginary monkish habits. It was to get rid of morbid fancies she walked over to Hazelwell when her husband took his departure for London. They got on well together, seldom quarrelled, although there was very little genuine love on her side.

About six months after Ulick Maynard left Hazelwell, Warren Courtly proposed to Irene. She declined the offer, but subsequently, acting mainly on her guardian's advice, she accepted him, and they were married the same year.

Redmond Maynard watched her moving about the room, and noticed how daintily she rearranged the various ornaments and chairs.

"There," she said, "that looks much better."

"I agree with you," he replied. "You have the artistic temperament strongly developed. By the way, have you done much painting during the past few months?"

"Yes, I have painted several pictures, but three out of every four I destroyed."

"They did not come up to your expectations?"

"No, and I do not care to keep inferior work. I think I have painted one that will please you."

"What is it—the subject?"

20

"A new departure for me. I have painted Random; I mean to give it you if you will accept it."

"That is good of you. I shall be delighted. Random shall have a prominent place in my study."

Random was a bright bay horse Redmond Maynard had given Irene on her marriage. He was a splendid hunter, either for lady or gentleman, and before Ulick left the horse had been his favourite.

Irene had been given the pick of the Hazelwell stable, and she selected Random because he had been Ulick's horse, and she thought, perhaps, his father would sell him now he was gone.

Random was duly sent over to Anselm Manor, and Irene vowed she would not part with him until Ulick came home, when she would hand him back to his rightful owner. She had ridden the horse in many a fast burst across country, and he carried her well. He was a safe, fearless jumper, and Irene was a splendid rider. When she appeared at a meet on Random, Sam Lane, the huntsman, thought, "We're in for it to-day; it will take the best of us all our time to keep up with Mrs. Courtly on Random." His surmise generally turned out correct, and on more than one occasion he and Irene were the only two in at the death. Many attempts had been made by sporting millionaires, American and otherwise, to secure Random, and a big figure would have been given for him, but Irene laughed at their offers, and said a shipload of gold would not buy him.

Random was sometimes the cause of dispute between Irene and her husband. Warren Courtly was ridiculously jealous of the horse. He would have scouted the idea that this feeling was engendered because Random had been Ulick Maynard's favourite horse, and yet Irene knew such to be the case. On more than one occasion he had suggested Random should be sold, or the Squire persuaded to make an exchange for him. His excuse was that the horse was not safe for a lady to ride, too much of a puller, and so on. Irene remained firm, and declined to entertain any ideas suggesting a parting with her favourite.

"You seem to care more for the horse than you do for me," he said, angrily.

She laughed, and said he must have a very poor opinion of himself if he thought she preferred Random.

"Mr. Maynard was kind enough to give him to me, and I mean to keep him. Don't let us quarrel about such a trifle. You would not like it if I asked you to give up your favourite hunter for a mere whim of mine."

"Has Warren become reconciled to Random?" asked the Squire. "I cannot understand his antipathy to the horse. Of course, he is anxious you should not run into danger, but Random is a very safe horse to ride—a more perfect fencer I have seldom seen."

"Warren has his likes and dislikes, and when he makes up his mind he seldom gives in. Random seems to have been his pet aversion ever since you gave him to me, and I do not think even now he would be at all sorry if he met with an accident, provided I came off scot free," laughed Irene.

"It is ridiculous. I begin to think I urged you to marry a monument of selfishness; I hope you will forgive me."

"You require no forgiveness. You provided me with a suitable husband and a good home. Warren is kind to me, and I have everything my own way. He is not a demonstrative man, but I feel sure he loves me, and he is not responsible for his restless disposition—that is inherited."

"And do you love him, Irene?" he asked.

She momentarily hesitated, and then said—

"Yes, I love him. We seem to understand each other now, although at first there was some restraint between us. I think we are quite as happy as the majority of married couples."

He was only half satisfied with her answer, but did not pursue the subject further.

"Is the painting of Random finished?" he asked.

"Yes, but not framed."

"May I send Bob over for it?"

"I will ride over myself if you will give me a mount," she said.

"The roads are very bad, will it be safe?"

22

"The horse can be 'roughed,' and I shall enjoy a ride in the keen morning air, it will brace me up."

"Very well, Irene. I will order Rupert to be saddled, he is the safest conveyance you can have in this weather."

CHAPTER IV

IRENE'S PAINTING

Irene mounted Rupert, and the Squire stood on the steps in front of the hall-door admiring the picture. The horse was a dark brown, nearly black, and stood out prominently against the snowy background. It was a sharp, crisp morning, the atmosphere clear, with a touch of frost in the air, and the sun shone brightly, the snow quivering in the light, glittering like myriads of crystals.

Rupert pawed the gravel in his eagerness to be going, and the Squire remarked, as he shook hands with Irene—

"You must come back as soon as you can. If you find the picture too cumbersome to carry leave it and we will send Bob for it."

"I can strap it on my back, I have a case made for the purpose. I often ride out with my sketching materials strapped on. You would take me for a tramp if you saw me walking about in my artist's costume," said Irene, laughing.

"A remarkably pretty tramp," said the Squire.

"Thanks, I will turn that compliment over in my mind as I ride to the Manor; it will be pleasant company for me."

Rupert set off at a brisk trot. He was at all times a sure-footed horse, and being roughed he had no difficulty in keeping his feet.

Irene's colour rose as the sharp breeze fanned her cheeks, and she was thoroughly enjoying her ride.

She went past the stud farm, and came across Eli Todd, who had been going his rounds.

Next to his runaway daughter, Janet, Eli Todd was devoted to Irene. He had known her from a child, had taught her to ride, and was proud of her accomplishment. He stood admiring her as she rode up.

"Good-morning, Eli; how are all your pets? I expect this weather does not suit some of them, but, of course, you have no foals yet?" said Irene.

"Everything is going on well," he replied; "but I am a bit anxious about old Honeysuckle."

"She must be getting on for twenty?" said Irene.

"Not far off that, Mrs. Courtly; in fact, I feel sure she is twenty, only it would not do to tell the Squire so, because he vows she is only eighteen, he won't hear of her being more," replied Eli, smiling.

"There is not much difference between eighteen and twenty; but why are you anxious about Honeysuckle, is there anything seriously amiss with her? I am going through Helton, and can ask Bard to call."

James Bard was the well-known county vet., and he lived at the little village of Helton, giving as his reason, "I prefer Helton; if I had my residence in the county town, people would be always demanding my services for all kinds of frivolous cases; it is a far way to Helton, and when they take the trouble to come for me I know the case is worth going to."

"No, thank you," replied Eli. "It is not necessary for Jim Bard to be called in, and I hope it will not be."

"Then what is it?" asked Irene.

"The old mare is very heavy in foal, and I'm mightily afraid the youngster will come into the world before the first of January, and there's no need to tell you that would be a misfortune," replied Eli.

"If he was born on December 31st it would mean he would be a year old on January 1st," said Irene, smiling.

"That's just it, and look what a disadvantage he would be at all his life. I may be wrong, but I assure you I am having a very anxious time."

"Have you told Mr. Maynard?"

"No, and please say nothing about it to him. He would only worry, and be constantly backwards and forwards between the house and the stables. You know how fond he is of the old mare."

"Honeysuckle is one of his great favourites, and no wonder; it is a good many years since she won the Oaks and the St. Leger for him. That is a fine painting he has of her in his study. I am afraid my poor effort will look very paltry beside it."

"Have you taken to painting horses?" asked Eli. He believed Irene capable of doing almost anything she put her hand to.

"I have tried to paint Random, and I am riding over to the Manor for the painting, as the Squire is anxious to see it."

"He'll make a grand picture; he's a fine subject to work on. There are not many hunters like him in the county. He was Mr. Ulick's favourite, and I was precious glad when you got him, for I was very much afraid the Squire would have sold him."

"You were very fond of Ulick, were you not, Eli?" she asked, in a soft tone of voice.

"To my mind there's not a man round these parts to compare with him."

"And you do not believe he ran away with Janet?"

"He never did that, I'll swear. You know he was not a man of that sort."

"Suspicion was, and still is, strong against him," she said.

"You cannot judge a man on suspicion, and in your heart you do not believe him guilty," he said.

"How can I believe otherwise? Who else could have done it?"

"I wish I could find out," he answered, vehemently. "I will some day, and then——"

"What then?"

"Something will happen. When I stand face to face with the man who stole my girl, he'll have to look to himself," said Eli, sternly.

"Do you think Janet will ever come back?" she asked.

"Yes, as sure as I believe Mr. Ulick will."

"I hope you will prove a true prophet," she replied. "If Ulick came back to Hazelwell and cleared himself, it would make a young man of the Squire. I should like to look round the stables, but I have no time now."

"Come when you like, I shall be only too pleased to show you the mares. Don't say anything to the Squire about Honeysuckle, please, Mrs. Courtly."

"I will not; I am discretion itself in such matters," laughed Irene, as she rode away.

It was four miles to the Manor, and when she arrived there she thought how cold and forbidding the old place looked when compared with Hazelwell.

The housekeeper was surprised to see her, and bustled about briskly.

"I am not going to remain long," said Irene. "I have merely come for a picture. I suppose Mr. Courtly has not returned?"

"No, but there is a letter for you, and it is his handwriting on the envelope."

Irene went into the morning-room and found some letters in the basket on the table.

She opened the one from her husband first. It was brief and to the point.

"Dear Irene,—I shall not be home for a week. If you feel lonely, go over to Hazelwell; I am sure the Squire will give you a warm welcome. Business must be attended to, you know, and the Anselm Estate takes a good deal of looking after. With love, I am, &c., Warren."

"Et cetera," said Irene to herself, smiling. "That's so like Warren. He is made up of et ceteras—it may mean much or little—it is so delightfully vague."

A faint odour of perfume was perceptible, and she wondered

27

where it came from. The letter was still in her hand, and as she wafted it carelessly about she discovered the paper was highly scented.

"That's not club paper," she thought. "Clubs are too prosaic to have scented paper about, besides, there is no heading; he must have written it at some friend's house. But why should it be a plain sheet with no address? And what a peculiar scent. My dear Warren, this requires some explanation; I will carefully preserve your eloquent epistle. Scented paper and legal affairs do not go well together, not in the management of estates, although I have no doubt breach of promise cases agree with it."

She folded the letter, and put it in the drawer of her writing-desk.

Two letters were addressed to Warren, and these she placed on one side; the fourth bore the London postmark, and she did not know the writing. The contents puzzled her. The letter was a request for money to enable the writer to tide over temporary difficulties. It was signed Felix Hoffman. She had never heard the name before. Why did the man write to her? How came he to know her address? It was a strange begging-letter, for no hint was given as to the writer's position, how he came to be in distress, why he wrote to her, or any information that was likely to induce her to accede to his request. The strangeness of the letter appealed to her. She firmly believed the man wanted money, also that he would repay her. There was no whining about it, none of the professional begging-letter writer's ways. Half-a-dozen lines, and no sum mentioned. The address sounded genuine—25, Main Street, Feltham, Middlesex. Where was Feltham? She took up Bradshaw's Guide, and found it was on the London and South-Western line, between Waterloo and Windsor. She had never heard of the place before, although she must have passed it on her way to Sunningdale for the Ascot week. Irene was given to making up her mind on the spur of the moment, and she did so in this case. She sat down at her desk, took her private cheque-book out, and sent the unknown and mysterious Felix Hoffman a cheque for five pounds.

"Easily imposed upon, I suppose that is what the majority of people would say; at any rate, if it is an imposition it is an uncommon one. I have a good mind to go up to London and on to Feltham just to spy out the land. I will ask the Squire about it. He will not call me a fool, he is far too polite, but he'll probably think I am one."

She sealed the letter and placed it in the postbag, locking it, and thus hiding her missive from prying eyes. Irene trusted her servants, but she understood human nature, and knew curiosity was well developed in the domestic maiden.

Passing into the room she used as a studio, she took the painting of Random from the easel and placed it in a more favourable light.

She criticised it, and was more than satisfied she had done the horse justice. The colouring was right, not hard, or harsh; the coat was not too glossy, yet it showed signs of health. The head was as perfect as it well could be. The left eye—the horse had his head turned three-parts round—was perhaps a shade too dull. She took up her palette, and with a couple of light touches altered it to her satisfaction.

"I think he will like it, and not merely because I have done it, but because it has merit."

She placed it in her portfolio, and adjusted the straps to suit her shoulders, so that it would not interfere with her riding. She rang the bell, and Mrs. Dixon, the housekeeper, appeared.

"Has anyone called, Dixon?"

"No; we need not look out for visitors in this weather."

Dixon was a privileged person; she had been in command at Anselm Manor long before Warren Courtly's mother died, and Irene declined to have her removed, although her husband would have been pleased to see the back of her.

Martha Dixon had a strong affection for Irene, although she would not abate a jot of her sternness or abrupt manner under any consideration. She also knew that Warren Courtly had been anything but a saint before he married, but that was none of her business.

"I suppose this is a gentle hint that I ought not to be riding about this weather?" said Irene, smiling.

Martha Dixon smiled back at her mistress and said, in a soft tone—

"If you take care of yourself it will do you no harm, and I know it's precious lonely at the Manor. How did you find the Squire?"

"He looks wonderfully well, but it was a bad night for him last night."

"Then he remembers; he has forgotten nothing?"

"And never will. He thinks Ulick will come back on the anniversary of the night he left home, and he has steeled himself to wait another year," said Irene.

"That minx Janet is at the bottom of it all. A regular little flirt; I have no patience with 'em," said Martha.

"Poor Janet, she has suffered for her wrongdoing, perhaps she is not to blame."

"Mr. Ulick ought to have packed her off somewhere and remained at home," she said.

"He was too much of a man to do that," said Irene. "Do you know, Dixon, I met Eli as I came here, and his faith in Ulick is as strong as ever?"

"It does him credit, but he knows different in his heart."

"You are mistaken; he believes Ulick is not guilty of wronging his daughter, I am sure of it."

"I wish it would come true," said Martha.

"I must go now," said Irene. "Please order my horse."

This being done, Martha Dixon fixed the picture firmly on Irene's back, and fastened the straps.

"The Squire will be pleased with that; it was Mr. Ulick's favourite horse."

"I believe that is why he was glad when I chose Random," said Irene, as she walked to the door and quickly mounted Rupert.

30

"If any letters come, shall I send them to Hazelwell?" asked Martha.

"No," replied Irene; then added quickly, as she thought of the mysterious Felix Hoffman, "on second thoughts, perhaps you had better do so, but I may ride over again in a day or two. Mr. Courtly writes that he will not be back for a week."

She rode quickly away, and Martha Dixon watched her until she was out of sight.

"I have nothing to say against Mr. Warren," muttered Martha, as she shut the door, "but I wish Mr. Ulick had not got into a mess. She'd have been happier with him, although I say it, as shouldn't."

CHAPTER V

HONEYSUCKLE'S FOAL

It was New Year's Eve, and Eli Todd was passing through a series of varying emotions. A stranger watching him might, with considerable excuse, have put him down as a lunatic. No sooner was he comfortably seated in his armchair by the cosy fire than he jumped up again suddenly, seized his hat, and dashed out into the wintry night.

After a quarter of an hour's absence he returned, settled down again, commenced to doze and, waking with a start, rushed out of the house in the same erratic manner as before.

The cause of these proceedings on the part of Eli was the mare, Honeysuckle. Never was a man placed in such a predicament, all on account of a mare, as Eli Todd on this occasion. It wanted four hours to midnight, and every moment the studmaster expected Honeysuckle's foal would come forth into the cold and heartless world an hour or two before the New Year. It was enough to drive him to despair. This would in all probability be Honeysuckle's last foal, but the Squire had already made up his mind that "what's last is best."

Blissfully ignorant was the Squire of the throes of anxiety his trusty servant was enduring. It was his firm belief that Honeysuckle would not foal until the middle of January at the earliest, and Eli had not undeceived him.

"I do wish you would keep still and not worry yourself," said Mrs. Marley. "It can do no good, the mare will get on quite as well without you; leave it to nature."

"Much you know about it," grumbled Eli. "Leaving it to nature is all very well, but you ought to know that nature requires a little assistance at times."

"You never take advice," she replied.

32

"I do when it is good," was the effectual reply.

Again Eli Todd opened the door, and a cold blast struck him in the face. A light was burning in Honeysuckle's box across the yard, and he plodded through the snow to it.

His head man was inside sitting in a chair, looking drowsy, and nodding.

Eli thought he had better go to bed, and said he would take his place.

"I'll call you if I want you," he said, and the man thanked him as he went out.

Eli sat in the chair watching the old mare and frequently looking at his watch. He had never wished time to fly so rapidly before.

Honeysuckle was restless, and from time to time looked at him with her big, soft eyes in a most pathetic way.

"I can't do anything for you, old girl," he said. "But you can oblige me very much by staving off the great event until the clock has struck twelve. After that the sooner you are over your trouble the better."

Another half hour passed, and still found Eli wakeful and on guard.

A slight noise outside aroused him, and he listened attentively. "It sounded like a man walking, perhaps Joe has come back. I know he is as anxious as I am about her," muttered Eli.

A knock on the door made him start, and he said—

"Who's there?"

No answer. It was mysterious at this hour of the night.

He asked the question again, and the reply was another rap.

Picking up his stick, he cautiously opened the door and peered out. He saw a man, muffled up; standing a yard or two away. Something about the figure seemed familiar to him, and a peculiar sensation passed through his body, making his pulses tingle with anticipation.

"Who are you, and what are you doing here?" he asked.

"Have you forgotten me, Eli?"

The studmaster started back, exclaiming—

"My God, it's Mr. Ulick!"

"Yes, it's me, none other; may I come in?"

For answer Eli dropped his stick, took him by both hands, and dragged him into the box.

Ulick Maynard unbuttoned his coat and unwound the scarf around his neck. He was a tall, handsome man, with a clear, open countenance. It was the face of a man to be trusted, if ever there was one.

"I am glad to see you, but it's a strange time to come," said Eli. "Are you going up to the house?"

"No," was the emphatic reply. "I shall never go back to Hazelwell until my father asks my pardon for the insult he put upon me."

"You don't know how he has suffered since you left," said Eli. "He sat up all night on Tuesday. You know what date it was?"

"Yes; I left home on that night two years ago."

"And Mrs. Courtly came over from the Manor and stayed with him," said Eli.

"Irene," he said softly.

"Yes, and she told me the Squire would be a young man again if you came back."

"Do they still believe I wronged your daughter?"

Eli made no reply, he thought it better to keep silent, for he would not tell a lie or deceive him.

34

"I see," said Ulick, bitterly. "I am still the black sheep, a disgrace to the name. And you, what do you think?"

"No need to ask me, Mr. Ulick. You know what I think. I never believed you guilty, and I never will, no, not even if Janet accused you, because she would be forced to it by the man who led her astray," said Eli.

Ulick took his hand and shook it heartily.

"Thank you, Eli," he said. "I give you my solemn word I did not wrong Janet. We may have flirted a trifle, as a man will do with a pretty girl, but I never injured her by word or deed. Is she at home still?"

Eli looked at him curiously. He evidently had no idea Janet left her home the same night he went away from Hazelwell.

"My girl has been away from me for two years."

It was Ulick's turn to look surprised.

"You thought it better to send her away, no doubt?"

"I did not send her away."

"She left her home, ran away from you?"

"That's what happened."

"When did she go?"

"The same night you did."

"Good heavens! No wonder my father still believes me guilty. No doubt he thinks I went with her," said Ulick.

"He came to my house in a towering passion the morning after she left, and when he found out she had gone he was very bitter against you both. He said words he ought not to have said, but I am sure he repented them afterwards."

"Have you heard anything of her?"

"No," replied Eli. "Not a line from her."

"I wonder who took her away? I'd give a good deal to find out," said Ulick.

"And so would I. She must be in London, I think; it is a good place to hide in," said Eli.

"So I find. A man can bury himself in London without much fear of recognition."

"Have you been in London since you left Hazelwell?" asked Eli.

"Most of the time. I very seldom came across anyone I know. You see, I have money of my own, independent of my father, so it enables me to live comfortably."

"And what has brought you down here?" asked Eli.

"Curiosity, a desire to see the old place, call it what you will. I wanted to have a chat with you, and hear how my father was going on," said Ulick.

"You had better go and see him. I am sure he has suffered enough by your absence."

"And do you not think I have suffered? And it makes it none the easier to bear because it is unjust. Have you ever suspected any one?"

"You mean about Janet?"

"Yes."

"I would rather not say. I have no proof, and if I am right it would cause even more trouble than the suspicion about you did."

"Then you have some idea who the man is?"

"I have, but we will not talk of that. If everything comes to light, well and good, but I am not going to be the one to cause more unhappiness."

"You ought to tell me. I have a right to know."

"Granted, but you must forgive me if I decline to say anything. This much I may tell you, that if what I suspect is true it will bring

36

shame and disgrace upon someone who is very dear to you," said Eli.

Ulick was astonished, and wondered if Eli really had any grounds for suspicion. He would think the matter over on his return to London; it might possibly afford him some clue. If he found out the real culprit he would be able to judge what was best to be done. It was no use questioning Eli further.

"Old Honeysuckle looks in rather a bad way," he said, changing the subject, for which Eli was very thankful.

Eli explained the situation to him, and Ulick, looking at his watch, said—

"It only wants half an hour to midnight; we have been talking a long time. I'll stay with you and see it through. There is no danger of the Squire suddenly coming down?"

"Not at this hour, I am glad to say. He thinks there is no cause for anxiety. But will you not come into the house? Mrs. Marley has gone to bed, and we shall not be disturbed," said Eli.

"Let us remain here until it is all over," replied Ulick, and he sat down on the straw.

"Take this chair," said Eli.

"I prefer to be here, it is more comfortable."

It was a quiet night, and the light wind was blowing from the village of Helton.

Honeysuckle was in considerable pain, and they both watched her with anxious eyes, knowing what a vast difference a few minutes would make.

"There's the church clock at Helton striking," said Eli, as he opened the door of the box. He gave a sigh of relief when the last stroke of twelve came. The bells pealed forth a welcome to the New Year, and the old year, with all its joys and sorrows, was gone for ever. What would the New Year bring forth?

"This was a curious way of seeing the Old Year out and the New Year in," said Ulick, smiling.

A quarter of an hour after midnight Honeysuckle's troubles were over, and a fine colt foal had come into the world almost at the sound of the church bells.

"We must make a note of this," said Eli, putting down the date and hour of foaling.

"I shall not forget it," said Ulick. "If there happened to be any dispute my father would be rather surprised if I was called as a witness."

"Go across to my cottage," said Eli. "I'll ring Joe up, there is no occasion for you to see him."

"I will wait outside the gate for you," said Ulick, as he went across the yard.

Leaving Joe in charge, with strict injunctions to call him at once if wanted, Eli hurried after Ulick, and, opening the door, led him into the room where he had an interview with Janet the night they both left home.

Ulick sank into a chair tired out, and soon fell asleep.

Eli stood looking on him with a sorrowful expression on his face.

"I wish he'd go and see the Squire," he said to himself. "There would be a reconciliation between them, I am sure; but Mr. Ulick is as proud and stubborn as his father when he knows he is in the right. He looks a trifle older, but not much. It's a blessing he does not lack for money. I wonder what he has been doing with his time, racing probably—it runs in the blood. He never was a great gambler; I hope he has not taken to it to kill time and drown his feelings."

Eli was accustomed to night watches, and did not go to sleep. He locked the door so that no one could intrude, and about four o'clock he roused Ulick and asked him to have something to eat.

"The cold and long walk made me drowsy," he said, with a yawn. "I acknowledge to feeling hungry, likewise thirsty. If you have any cold meat; that will do, and some of your noted beer."

"I suppose you wish to keep this visit a secret?" asked Eli.

"Yes; it has done me good to run down to the old place. I shall

38

try and find out Janet when I get back to town. You have no objection, I suppose?"

"On the contrary, I hope you will find her. If you do, try and induce her to come home."

"I'll bring her myself if I can," said Ulick. "They think we went away together, so we may as well return together; but she will have to give me the name of the man who has caused all the trouble."

He ate ravenously, and Eli was pleased to see him make such a hearty meal.

"I must be going now," said Ulick. "You will not tell anyone I have been here."

"No. Which way are you going?"

"I shall walk to Haydon Station and catch the early train to London. I got out there; there is a new station-master, he does not know me."

"That's more than ten miles," said Eli.

"It will do me good. I have not done much country walking lately."

"Will you leave me your address in town, I will take care no one sees it?" asked Eli.

Ulick wrote on a sheet in his pocket-book, and handed it to Eli, saying, "That address will always find me, no matter whether I am in London or otherwise. I always have my letters sent on, even if I am only away for a few days at a race meeting."

"Then you go in for racing?" said Eli, smiling.

"Yes, I have attended many meetings since I left Hazelwell."

"Do you bet?"

Ulick laughed, as he replied, "Sometimes, but I know too much about it to risk large sums. Between you and me, Eli, I own a couple of horses, one I daresay you have heard of, his name is the Saint."

"You own the Saint!" exclaimed Eli; "why, he was about the best of the two-year-olds last season."

"He was, and he will not be far off being the best of the three-year-olds this season. I bought him for a reasonable figure. Of course, you know his breeding: by Father Confessor out of Hilda. I hope to win some good races with him. He runs in the assumed name of Mr. Lanark. I hope when brighter days have dawned he will come to Hazelwell. It would rather surprise the Squire if he knew he belonged to me."

Ulick went into the hall and put on his coat.

"We might ride part of the way," said Eli.

"It's better for me to walk," replied Ulick, and added, "I will let you know if I hear anything of Janet, and will try and persuade her to come home."

"Thank you, Mr. Ulick, and if you do come across her, tell her home is the best place for her, and that I shall never remind her of what has happened."

"And you still have faith in me?" asked Ulick, smiling, as he shook hands.

"Yes, and always shall have, as I told you before," said Eli, who watched him until he disappeared in the darkness, and wondered at the strange chance that brought him to Hazelwell the night Honeysuckle's foal was born.

CHAPTER VI

A WILY YOUNG MAN

In a small, but comfortably-furnished house at Feltham, lived Mrs. Hoffman and her son, Felix. She was not a widow, but her husband had left her some years before. At that time her son was seventeen, now he was five-and-twenty, and a sore trial and trouble to her. Felix Hoffman was one of many men who prefer idleness to work, and he took good care not to find any suitable employment. It troubled his mother that he was seldom short of money. How did he obtain it? Not by work of any kind, of that she was certain. Once or twice she questioned him as to how he made sufficient to supply his wants, which were by no means few or inexpensive, but he always flew into a passion on such occasions, and his attitude became so threatening that she forebore to make further inquiries.

Felix Hoffman was not bad looking. He had a Jewish cast of features, black curly hair, and a fierce moustache of the same colour. His eyes were dark brown, shifty and uncertain, and when he conversed he seldom looked his companion in the face.

He did not resemble his mother in the least; she was English, and married Milas Hoffman when quite a girl. Had she been more experienced in the ways of the world he would have had but little chance of winning her. A few months after their marriage she found out her mistake. Milas Hoffman called himself a travelling jeweller. He certainly went about the country with a case packed with glittering ornaments, which he disposed of on most advantageous terms to servant girls, young grooms, and others of the same class in different countries. His profits were large, and he made a very fair income out of the gullibility of his customers. He became more daring in his transactions, and at last came within the grasp of the law. Not wishing to face the charges of swindling brought against him, he left England, and his wife had never heard of him since. She did not mourn over his desertion. She had sufficient money by her to carry on for a time, and she fixed her hopes upon her son Felix. They were doomed to be rudely shattered when he coolly told her

41

there were plenty of ways of making money without working for it. What those ways were he failed to tell her, but it saddened her to see that he was right, and he drew supplies from sources she felt sure she could not approve of.

Felix Hoffman met many men in London in very different positions in life to himself. He was a frequenter of racecourses, one of the undesirables whose presence gives the sport a bad name, and its enemies a handle wherewith to pump obloquy upon all connected with it, the just and the unjust. At first he was a bookmaker's tout, and rushed about the ring watching the fluctuation of the odds, scenting out stable commissions and repeating the same to his employer with lightning speed. It was seldom the bookmaker was let in for a big bet "over the odds" when Felix Hoffman was hovering about with hawk-like keenness. The said bookmaker, whose sham diamonds were the envy of the uninitiated, became so impressed with the fertile resources of Felix Hoffman that he actually ventured to take him into partnership "in the book." This was a grave mistake, for in a very short time the versatile Felix had transformed the firm, and his name alone figured on the bag and tickets. The members of Tattersall's smiled; many of them had seen these mysterious changes before and knew what it meant. Felix Hoffman, in his turn, made a mistake. He handed over the "bag" to two men he fancied he could trust, and proceeded to back horses on his own account. He saw no reason why, with his skill in scenting out commissions and spotting genuinely-backed horses, he should not be able to lay the losers and back the winners. Better men than Felix had endeavoured to accomplish this feat before, and come lamentably to grief, and he followed them into the same quandary. It puzzled Felix not a little to find out the cause of his failure. He had not yet learned that to be successful on the turf a man must be either a backer or a layer, but not both, and in the one capacity a good share of luck must be his to succeed.

Warren Courtly was fond of racing, especially "chasing," and during the off-season he was frequently seen at meetings round London. Even the attractions of the hunting field could not, on many occasions, lure him from the racecourse. Irene knew he frequented such places, but she had no idea of the extent of his gambling transactions, or they would have appalled her. She thought his statement that the Anselm Manor estates required a good deal of looking after was an excuse for his visits to London, but, as a matter of fact, he was correct in his assertion. Everything he could mortgage he did, and even the Manor itself had sundry charges upon it, which he found it difficult to meet. The racecourse is a rare levelling ground, and men of very different types fraternise together with a freedom never seen elsewhere. Warren Courtly had noticed Felix Hoffman's energy in ferreting out information, and on more than one occasion had taken the trouble to find out whether he was right or wrong. In this way he gathered that his advice was generally good. He approached him one day at Hurst Park, and asked his advice about Milander in a hurdle race.

Felix Hoffman was not at all surprised at a stranger speaking to him about such matters. He eyed Warren Courtly over, and came to the conclusion it would pay him to tell him all he knew. As luck would have it, he did know Milander was a very fair thing for the hurdle race.

"I'll make it worth your while if it wins," said Warren.

"What will you put me on?"

"I will lay you the odds to a fiver."

"Milander has a very good chance. Dyer rides him, and he told me, bar accident, he would win. I think you can back him for a good stake."

"Meet me here after the race," said Warren, and walked out of the paddock into the ring.

"He's a real swell," thought Felix. "He may come in useful."

Milander won comfortably, and started at the remunerative odds of five to one. Warren Courtly won a good stake, and handed Felix "a pony," the winnings on the five pounds he put on for him.

"I'd give Dyer something, sir, if I were you," said Felix. "He's not a bad sort, and generally tells me when he has a chance."

"Give him this," said Warren, handing Felix a ten-pound note.

"Shall I see you again, sir?"

"I am often at these meetings. If you know anything, come and tell me, and I will see you are a gainer thereby."

It was in this way Warren Courtly became acquainted with Felix Hoffman, who later on helped him in another way, which did not redound to his credit, and which eventually gave that wily young man a hold over the master of Anselm Court.

Mrs. Hoffman was surprised one day when her son brought Warren Courtly down to Feltham. She wondered how Felix became acquainted with him, and still more why his friend condescended to associate with him. She knew her son was not at all a desirable companion for a man of Warren Courtly's stamp.

Felix introduced him as Mr. Warren. "A gentleman I have frequently met on the racecourse, mother; he wishes to consult you on a private matter, and I hope you will agree to his request."

Mrs. Hoffman was surprised, but expressed her readiness to hear what he had to tell her.

"It is rather a delicate matter," commenced Warren, when Felix left the room; "the fact of the matter is, I am anxious to find a comfortable home for my wife until my father can be informed of our marriage. He is very much set against it because the lady is hardly in the same set as ourselves. I have married for love, but that is no reason why I should forfeit the many advantages I now have, and which I should certainly lose if my father found out I was married. My wife is young and pretty, and would, I am sure, cause very little trouble in a house. I asked your son if he knew of any place where I could leave her, in or near London, and he said he had no doubt his mother would be pleased to have her, and he was quite certain would make her comfortable. If you have no objection, Mrs. Hoffman, I should like my wife to have rooms here, and I am sure I could rely upon you to treat her kindly, and be a companion to her."

Mrs. Hoffman was not at all displeased at this proposal, but she foresaw one danger, and that was Felix. She knew him to be utterly unscrupulous, and feared his influence over a young married woman living apart from her husband, for that was what it meant. However, she would take very good care he had no opportunities of making himself objectionable to her.

Warren Courtly noticed the hesitation, and said, "I do not think there will be any trouble over the terms. I know very little about these matters, but if you will make a suggestion I will consider it."

Mrs. Hoffman had no intention of asking too little. Her experience of life had taught her much, and she had her doubts as to the truth of the story she had heard. Still, that was none of her business, and she meant to do her duty by the girl when she came to her house.

"Would three guineas a week be too much, sir? There may be a few extras, which I suppose you would not mind paying for?"

"That is reasonable," said Warren, who had expected a higher figure, "and I hope you will do all in your power to make Mrs. Warren comfortable."

"I can safely promise you that, and that I shall be very pleased to have someone in the house, for my son is generally away from home. When may we expect you, sir?"

Warren named the date, and she replied—

"That is quite close to Christmas. Shall you stay here during that week, if so I will prepare for you?"

"I am sorry to say I shall be away; my father will expect me to be at home with the rest of the family," said Warren.

In due course, Warren arrived at Mrs. Hoffman's house at Feltham with Janet Todd, and she had been there two years living under the name of Mrs. Warren.

Seven or eight months after he had found Janet a home with Mrs. Hoffman, Warren married Irene Carstone, and considered he had done his duty by Janet, and that this discreditable action in his life was closed.

It troubled him when he heard Ulick Maynard was looked upon as the wrongdoer, but he had not the manliness or the courage to confess, and thus place the blame upon his own shoulders.

It was a strange coincidence, he thought, that the Squire should have made this accusation against Ulick on the same night he had planned to take Janet away. He had not much difficulty in persuading her to go, and he knew she was fully convinced he would marry her. This did not trouble him much, his anxiety was to get her away from Hazelwell, because he had at that time made up his mind to marry Irene, if she would have him.

Fate played into his hands, and worked everything smoothly for him. When he heard from Janet that Ulick had been at her father's, and told her the Squire had accused him of being the cause of her misfortune, Warren was astounded. He saw at once how Janet's flight would confirm the Squire's charge, and that everyone would believe she had left her home with Ulick.

"What did he say to you?" asked Warren.

Janet hung her head, and her cheeks became crimson.

"Tell me what he said," Warren asked, sharply.

"He was very angry, and said I deserved to be thrashed for bringing disgrace upon my father; as for myself, it was no more than I deserved. He asked me who had got me into trouble."

"You did not tell him?" said Warren, anxiously.

"How can you ask such a question? Of course I did not tell him."

"That's a good girl, Janet; you must always keep our secret."

"That depends upon how you treat me," she replied, and at this answer Warren Courtly commenced to see it might not be all plain sailing with her.

"Did Mr. Maynard tell you he was suspected of being the cause of your trouble?"

"Yes, and I offered to write to his father and tell him it was untrue, but he was very angry and forbade me doing so, saying his father ought to have known him better, and that he must find out the truth for himself," said Janet.

Warren was relieved at this. He knew Ulick Maynard had a proud, stubborn disposition, and that his father's suspicions would sting him to the quick. It was not at all likely he would ask Janet to prove his innocence, and when she was at Feltham he would have but little chance of finding her, even if he changed his mind.

They arrived in London, and went from Waterloo to Feltham.

"Remember, you are Mrs. Warren," he said, "and do not let anyone find out where you come from. Mrs. Hoffman you will like, but her son is a scamp, and you will do well to avoid him."

Mrs. Hoffman soon grew very fond of Janet, and the girl reciprocated the motherly feelings thus shown. She was not unhappy, but she would have been more contented had Warren allowed her to write to her father and tell him all was well with her. This, however, he strictly forbade; he did not wish her to have any communication with Hazelwell.

The first serious quarrel took place when Warren told her he was to marry Irene Carstone.

Janet wept, and then flew into a rage, vowing she would write to her father, the Squire, and Irene, and confess all. He dare not leave her for a week, and during that time he used all his persuasive powers to calm her, and at times resorted to threats, which she only laughed at.

Eventually he took Mrs. Hoffman into his confidence, and discovered that she had suspected the truth all along.

"I wish you would use your influence with her," he said; "I am quite willing to make her a good allowance, and also settle a sum of money upon her, provided she holds her tongue."

Mrs. Hoffman promised she would do all that lay in her power to bring Janet to a proper frame of mind. She really liked her, and thought she was far happier as she was than if she had married Warren.

She succeeded in her endeavour, but Janet was mercenary when it came to terms with Mr. Courtly. She was determined to have adequate remuneration for all she had lost, and the deception he had practised on her. He grumbled at her demands, but she was firm, and as there was no other way out of the difficulty, except exposure, he gave in.

Janet knew her power over him, and his marriage with Irene materially increased it.

"I wonder what she would do if she knew all?" thought Janet.

CHAPTER VII

SELLING HIS HERITAGE

It was hardly to be expected that Janet should remain under the roof of Mrs. Hoffman without attracting the attention of her unscrupulous son, and at last Felix Hoffman annoyed her so persistently that his mother gave him to understand if he did not desist he would be forbidden the house. Janet hated the sight of him, and seldom answered his questions. This annoyed him, and offended his pride, of which he possessed a ridiculous quantity. One day, when Janet was out, he came across a letter she had carelessly left on her table, and without scruple picked it up and read it. The contents did not afford him much gratification, but the heading to the paper gave food for reflection. Anselm Manor, Rushshire, sounded well, and the letter was signed Warren.

"Warren what? He must have another name," thought Felix. "I should like to know what it is."

He set to work to find out, and was not long before he succeeded. Warren Courtly was well known amongst sporting men, and Felix soon discovered who and what he was.

He chuckled to himself as he thought what a commotion it would cause if Mrs. Courtly knew about Janet Todd's connection with her husband. He foresaw a profitable harvest from this source, but had no intention of putting Warren Courtly on his guard at present.

He had written many begging letters in the course of his life, and several of them had proved effective. It occurred to him it would be a neat stroke of business to write to Mrs. Courtly for assistance, and after several attempts he decided to dispatch the one already alluded to.

It reached Irene safely, with the result that Felix was enriched by five pounds. He was quite proud of this achievement, for he had doubts as to the success of his missive.

He wrote back thanking her, and repeating that he would refund the money at some future date.

This was how Irene came to have a knowledge of Felix Hoffman. His reply was sent on to Hazelwell, and she decided to show both letters to the Squire.

"I hope you will not think me very foolish," she said, as she handed him the letters; "you will gather from them what has taken place."

Redmond Maynard read them, and said—

"This man, whoever he is, must be a clever rogue, it is a form of begging-letter writing I have never seen before. I do not blame you for sending the money, although had you consulted me I should have felt more inclined to hand over the matter to the police. You must not send him any more money," said the Squire.

"Do you think he will write for more?"

"Most decidedly, especially as his first letter was such a success."

"I had thought of going to Feltham the next time I am in London, and finding out where he lives and the kind of man he is," she said.

"You must not do anything of the kind. There is no telling where he is; at any rate, you must not venture there alone," he replied.

"It is merely from a desire to gratify my curiosity that I wish to go. I am sure no harm will come of it."

The Squire shook his head, as he replied—

"The letter has cost you five pounds, let the matter drop and think no more about it."

"Feltham is not far from Kempton Park," said Irene. "I wonder if Warren knows anything about the place?"

"Probably. Ask him when he returns home," said the Squire. "By the way, Irene, I had almost forgotten it is New Year's Day. We are not a very jolly household for the occasion, but we must not

49

commence another year with gloomy thoughts and melancholy countenances."

"I hope this year will bring Ulick home again," she said.

"So do I, with all my heart," said the Squire. "There's Eli coming up the walk, I wonder what he wants."

"Shall I tell Bob to send him in when he arrives?" she asked.

"Yes, do, Irene."

Eli Todd came into the room, and wished them a cheery Happy New Year. "We have made a good start at the stud, although I had a terribly anxious time of it," he said.

"Made a good start, what do you mean?" said the Squire. "There are no foals yet?"

"Only one," replied Eli, smiling, "and he was precious near being born before midnight. As luck would have it, he came into the world a quarter of an hour after, so that is all right."

"But there was no mare due to foal so early," remarked the Squire.

"Only old Honeysuckle," said Eli, with a smile.

"You mean to tell me the old mare has a foal? I was certain it would be the middle of the month before that event came off," said the Squire.

"I knew you were wrong, but I did not contradict you," replied Eli.

"Then if you knew I was wrong, it was your business to tell me, and you ought to have done so," said the Squire.

Eli was a privileged servant, and although always respectful to the Squire, occasionally answered him bluntly.

"It is not an easy matter to contradict you, Squire; you generally like to have your own way," said Eli.

Irene laughed, and said she must certainly side with him in his remark.

50

"That is rather hard upon me," replied the Squire. "I had no idea I was so obstinate."

"Oh, but you are," laughed Irene, "and once you have made up your mind you stick to it through thick and thin."

"That is about a correct summing up of the situation," said Eli.

"What sort of a youngster is it?" asked the Squire.

"Very promising, so far as I can judge at this stage; he ought to make a good one."

"Do let us go and see him," said Irene.

The Squire walked to the window and looked out. The snow still lay deep upon the ground, but it was hard and crisp, and afforded good walking.

"I think we may venture," he said. "Will you come, Irene?"

"With pleasure, I will not be more than a few minutes putting on my things." She left the room, and returned enveloped in a seal-skin jacket, trimmed with heavy sable, and a toque to match. She looked very attractive, and the Squire glanced at her admiringly. Eli Todd thought he had never seen a prettier woman, and wondered how Ulick could have been so foolish as to leave the way clear for Warren Courtly to win her.

They thoroughly enjoyed the walk in the brisk, frosty air, and when they arrived at the stud farm Eli took them to Honeysuckle's box.

He quietly opened the door, and, stepping inside, they saw a pretty sight. The mare was standing sideways to them, and as they entered the foal looked at them with big, inquiring eyes. He sidled up close to his mother, and playfully pushed her with his nose. He was a well-made colt, long on the leg, and with a beautiful head and well-shaped body.

The Squire eyed him critically for several minutes, and then said—

"He ought to make a good one, there is plenty of room for him to fill out and develop. I am glad Honeysuckle has thrown such a good one, it will probably be her last."

51

"I thought you would like him," said Eli.

Irene went up to him and patted him gently. The colt was not at all alarmed, and sniffed at her jacket and fur with evident relish.

"He's a dear little fellow," she said, "and I hope he will win a good race or two for you. I should like to see him win."

"You may have that pleasure next year," said the Squire, "that is if he goes on all right; so many promising foals turn out badly, one never knows what may happen."

Bersak put his head in the door, and the colt started back in alarm. It was his first introduction to another animal, and he evidently regarded Bersak as some wild savage beast of prey. Honeysuckle turned round, and looked straight at the intruder, but she and Bersak were friends and had met many times before.

Eli thought of the scene the previous night, and wished he could tell the Squire he had seen Ulick. He had given his word not to mention the visit, and therefore his lips were sealed.

"We will walk through the plantation on the way home," said the Squire, "it is a short cut, and I feel I shall be ready for luncheon when we get in."

They set off at a brisk pace, Bersak following at their heels. It was a pleasant walk, and hares and rabbits frequently ran across their path, while the pheasants strutted about proudly, their brilliant plumage affording a sharp contrast to the snow.

After luncheon the Squire had his usual nap, and Irene looked over the various papers and magazines.

A paragraph caught her eye, and she read it with feelings of wonder and amazement. It was to the effect that Mr. Warren Courtly, of Anselm Manor, had disposed of Holme Farm for the sum of ten thousand pounds, and this was instanced as another proof of the decreased value of land.

"Sold the Holme Farm, there must be some mistake!" thought Irene, and read the paragraph again.

"He never mentioned anything about it to me, and I know of no reason why he should sell it. I wonder where these rumours originate; they have no business to insert them in the paper until they ascertain whether they are correct."

She was troubled over it, although she did not believe it to be true. The Holme Farm was one of the best on the Anselm estate, and even if Warren had been compelled to sell it, she thought he might have given the Squire the first refusal. She failed to understand the meaning of it, and was still puzzling over the matter when the Squire awoke and looked at her through his half-closed eyes.

He saw something had disturbed her, and, sitting up in his chair, inquired the cause.

"There is an announcement in the paper I cannot understand," she said. "This is it."

He read the paragraph and said, "What an abominable statement to make. It must be some other farm of that name, and Warren's name has been inadvertently inserted as that of the owner."

He looked at it again, and saw it was an announcement made by the auctioneers who sold the property. This made the matter more serious, the sellers would not be likely to make such a mistake.

"Warren would never have sold it without telling me he was about to do so," said Irene.

"He has done a very foolish thing if he has sold it," said the Squire. "He cannot possibly be short of money with the income he has. Ten thousand pounds is a ridiculous sum for the Holme Farm, it ought to be worth five thousand more at least. He will explain what it all means when he returns home."

Notwithstanding he spoke confidently, the Squire had his misgivings. He had heard vague rumours from his brother magistrates, when he met them as chairman of the county bench and of the quarter sessions, that all was not well with Warren Courtly. He paid very little attention to the statements, treating them as so much idle gossip, but they came home to him forcibly now. He had heard that Warren Courtly had been going the pace on the racecourse and gambling heavily, but he thought Warren quite capable of looking after himself. They passed a somewhat quiet afternoon and evening, for the announcement disturbed them both, and Irene was anxious for the next morning to come, in the hope it might bring her some explanation from her husband.

It was quite true that Warren Courtly had sold the Holme Farm for ten thousand pounds, and the bulk of the money received from it went to pay his debts. He was in no very enviable frame of mind when he stepped into the Windsor train at Waterloo on his way to Feltham to see Janet. He was heartily sick and tired of her, and of the deception he had to practise in connection with her. Moreover, Janet was becoming troublesome, and, what was still worse, homesick. She was constantly imploring him to allow her to return to her father, promising to keep his secret and never to breathe a word about their intimacy. Warren Courtly would not hear of it. He knew of Eli Todd's great affection and devotedness to Ulick, and felt certain he would extract the truth from Janet if she lived with him again. He had wronged Irene, and deceived her, but he meant to shield her from the consequences of his folly at any cost. She must never know that he had been cowardly enough to allow Ulick to lie under the ban of a false accusation.

He left the train at Feltham, and walked to Mrs. Hoffman's.

Janet shook hands with him as an ordinary acquaintance; there was no love between them now, whatever there had been a couple of years ago. The more she saw of him and learned his nature, the more she despised him.

"You are looking well," he said, "the world is treating you better than me."

"Is it?" she answered, carelessly. "I am very unhappy, I want to go home again. I cannot rest until Mr. Ulick's name is cleared. It is a shame he should suffer for your fault."

"My fault and yours," he said, angrily. "You always lay all the blame at my door."

"And that is where it ought to be. I was a fool ever to trust you."

"I have done all I can for you, more than I can afford."

She laughed as she replied—

"That is nice talk for the owner of Anselm Manor."

54

"It is true nevertheless. I have sold the Holme Farm to pay my debts."

"I don't believe it."

"Read that," he said, and handed her the paper with an account of the sale.

"Ten thousand pounds!" she exclaimed. "That is a lot of money. I am rather short of cash, you must give me some."

"You had twenty pounds last month."

"And I want twenty more now."

"You cannot have it."

"Then you must take the consequences," she said.

"What shall you do?"

"Pack up my things, go down to Helton, see my father, and tell the truth," she replied.

"You dare not, no one would believe your story."

"One person would, I am certain," she answered.

"Your father?"

"Probably, but I meant your wife," said Janet.

"You dare not speak to her of such things," he said, angrily.

"And why not? She has every right to know the truth."

"If I give you the money will you hold your tongue?" he asked.

"Yes, until I require more," was her reply.

He gave her twenty pounds, thankful to be able to stave off the evil day, hoping in the meantime to find some way out of his difficulties.

CHAPTER VIII

WARREN'S RETURN

Warren Courtly returned home during the week, and Irene was at the Manor to receive him. She did not welcome him with her usual heartiness, and he expected there was something wrong.

"You have been away a long time," she said. "I expected you home last week. Your business must have been very important."

"It was," he replied, "and I have not finished it. I shall have to go to London again soon."

"I will accompany you," she said; "I have not been to London for some time."

"As you wish. I shall be glad of your society. Have you been staying with the Squire?"

"Yes, and we have managed to pass the time pleasantly. I took him the picture of Random, and he was delighted with it; he has it in his study. We were very much surprised to see an announcement in the paper that you had sold the Holme Farm, but I suppose it is incorrect?"

"I am sorry to say it is correct. I had to sell it, Irene, I was in difficulties."

"You, in difficulties!" she exclaimed. "How is that possible, you have a large income?"

"I have been gambling, and owed more than I could pay. So I thought the best way would be to sell Holme Farm and clear them all off. I shall be more cautious next time, you may be sure."

"You might have told me how matters stood," she said, reproachfully. "And if you were compelled to sell the Farm, why did you not offer it to the Squire, he would have given you a better price than that for it?"

56

"I had no idea he would buy it; he is always grumbling about land, and saying it is no good investing in it."

"He said Holme Farm was worth five thousand more than you accepted for it, and I believe he would have given it."

He was angry with himself when he heard this, but he knew the real reason he had not offered it to the Squire was that he was ashamed to do so. As he looked at Irene, he recognised her beauty more clearly than he had ever done before. He felt he was dealing her blow after blow, and the worst was yet to come. It made him desperate when he thought of Janet, and the trouble she could cause. Why had he been such a fool to fall into the toils of such a minx? He hated her name, and it was sacrilege to think of her in the presence of Irene. As for Irene she was depressed and uneasy at her husband's statement. If he was compelled to sell the Holme Farm, others might follow, and the estate gradually dwindle down to small proportions. It was not a bright prospect after only eighteen months of married life. She saw he was worried and troubled, and did not look himself.

"Are you feeling unwell?" she asked.

"No, why?"

"Because you do not look in your usual health; if you have any trouble, Warren, I wish you would confide in me, and I might possibly help you. It will be far better for me to hear it from you than from any outsiders, and you know what gossips people are."

He felt a strong impulse to tell her everything even to confess his fault with Janet, and how he had allowed suspicion to rest upon Ulick, but he dare not do it. He knew she would never forgive him, although she might condone his failings. If an outsider made her acquainted with the fact it would be far worse, but he must risk that.

"I have nothing to tell you," he said. "It troubled me to have to part with the farm, but I saw no other way out of the difficulty."

"I can quite understand that," she replied. "As it was necessary for you to do it, we will say no more about it; but I expect the Squire will pull you over the coals," she added, with a smile.

Next morning a thaw set in, and the pure white landscape

quickly changed to a dull, leadened colour. The melting snow dripped from the roof in a monotonous splash, the trees were wet and dismal, and the ground was a mass of sticky slush and mud. The sky was dark and lowering, and the effect depressing.

They both felt the effects of the change at breakfast time. Irene was naturally of a bright disposition, and tried to cheer her husband's drooping spirits, but with ill-success.

"Honeysuckle had a colt foal half an hour after midnight on New Year's Day," she said. "That was a slice of luck, and Eli had a very anxious time until he was born."

"What an extraordinary thing," he said. "The Squire would be pleased. What kind of a colt is he?"

"A good one I should say; we saw him the same day, and he pleased both the Squire and Eli."

"I must have a look at him," he replied; then, glancing out of the window, went on: "There is nothing more miserable than a thaw; I shall be glad when all the snow is gone, and there is a chance of hunting again."

"It will be a treat to be in the saddle after such a long spell," she replied. Then, changing the subject, she said, "I had a peculiar letter when you were away. I showed it to the Squire, and he thought it was written by a clever rogue. My impression was that the man was genuinely in want of a small loan, but how he came to write to me I do not know. Here is the letter and his reply to my note."

Warren Courtly took it carelessly, but no sooner did he see the handwriting than he hastily turned to look at the signature, and when he saw "Felix Hoffman" the letter fell upon the table and he sank back into his chair, his face white and drawn.

Irene was surprised and alarmed at the effect it produced, and said—

"What is the matter, Warren? Is it the letter causes you anxiety? Do you know the man?"

He made no answer, but took the letter and read it, wondering how it came about that Felix Hoffman should have discovered who he was and have the audacity to write to his wife. Janet must have confided in him, that was the only solution he arrived at, and he vowed she should suffer for her betrayal. These brief minutes, when his wife's eyes were upon him, noting every change and movement, were the worst he had ever spent in his life.

"Do you know the man?" she asked, again.

"Yes, I know him."

"Who is he?"

"A racecourse sharper, a scoundrel, an unprincipled blackguard," said Warren, savagely.

"Then how is it you know him?" she asked.

"We meet many undesirable people on racecourses; he is one of the most undesirable."

"But you have no necessity to associate with such men."

"They are useful sometimes; even the man Hoffman has given me good information."

"If he is such a man as you describe, I should be ashamed to be seen with him. How dare he write to me?" she said, angrily.

"It was a gross piece of impertinence," replied Warren, "for which he shall pay dearly. Leave me to deal with him, Irene."

"He ought to be thrashed," she said.

"He shall be, and he will not forget it as long as he lives. You were very foolish to send the money."

"The Squire said the letter ought to have been handed over to the police."

"It was a blessing it was not," thought Warren.

It was a rapid thaw, and at the end of the week not a vestige of snow was to be seen, except in some shaded corner where the sunlight never crept in, and where the overhanging cavern kept off the dripping water.

Warren Courtly rode over to Hazelwell, and did not receive a very hearty greeting from Redmond Maynard.

They looked at Honeysuckle's foal, and Warren pronounced it one of the best she had had. Eli Todd, he fancied, treated him in a somewhat off-hand manner. Surely he did not suspect anything, he could not unless Janet had written to him.

Everything jarred upon him, his nerves were disordered, and he felt irritable and out of sorts. He dreaded an exposure, and felt it was gradually coming. He knew what the Squire's wrath would be when he found out Ulick had been unjustly suspected, as he must do sooner or later.

"Tell him all and get rid of the burden," whispered conscience. He dare not, and yet it would have been the best way out of the sea of trouble into which he was floundering.

In the Squire's study hung the painting of Random, and he pointed it out to Warren with pride, and said—

"Irene has done it splendidly; it is lifelike. I never saw a picture of a horse more natural. You ought to be proud of your wife, she does many things, and does them all well."

"I am proud of her," said Warren, in a half-hearted tone that irritated the Squire, who of late had been constantly blaming himself for being the cause of Irene throwing herself away upon Warren Courtly.

"She is the best woman I know, and her heart is in the right place. Confound it, Warren, you have no right to leave her alone as you do, it is not fair to her. Why don't you take her up to London, if you really have to go to town so often?"

"I will next time," said Warren, lamely. He seemed at a loss for words, and the Squire thought he had a shame-faced look.

"He's been up to some devilment, I'm sure of it," he thought. "By Jupiter, if he's done anything to trouble Irene's peace of mind he'll find he has me to reckon with."

"Your journey to London does not seem to have benefited you much," said the Squire.

"I hate town," grumbled Warren.

"Then why go there?"

"Because it is so deuced dull at the Manor when there is no hunting on."

"The selfish beggar," thought the Squire, as he said aloud, "And do you not think it is dull for Irene when you are away?"

"She is generally at Hazelwell, and you are excellent company, Squire."

"Am I? Much you know about it. Let me tell you if it had not been for Irene I should have had a fit of the blues that would have got the best of me a few nights back. Perhaps you can imagine what night it was?" said the Squire.

"No, I cannot; but, anyway, I am glad she was here to cheer you up. I told her to ride over and see you."

"Have you forgotten what happened over two years ago?"

He could not pretend to misunderstand, although they were getting on rather dangerous ground.

"You mean the night Ulick left home?"

"Yes, and I sat up all that night, and I shall sit up every night when it comes round, year by year, until he returns home again."

"Then you have changed your mind?" said Warren.

"I have forgiven him, but he must prove his innocence, and I am beginning to believe he will. Something tells me he will," he said, as he looked at Warren in a way that made him feel very uncomfortable, and yet he knew nothing had been found out—at present.

"Ulick was hardly the sort of man one would have expected to get into such a mess," said Warren.

"You are right; that is what I cannot understand," replied the Squire, thinking at the same time Warren Courtly was a much more likely man to do so.

"Irene told me you thought I was foolish to accept ten thousand for the Holme Farm," said Warren.

"And I still think so. Why did you sell it?"

61

"I had to, I owed a lot of money."

"Betting?"

"Mostly, but I am out of the mire now, and intend to keep so," he replied.

"A good resolution. Why did you not offer me the Farm? I would have given you a better price for it."

"Because, to tell you the truth, I was ashamed to."

"You ought to have come to me, Warren," said the Squire, kindly, as he placed one hand on his shoulder. "I gave you Irene, and you ought to trust me. She was confided to my care by my old friend, Carstone, and I do not want to think I have made a mistake in placing her happiness in your hands. You do not look easy in your mind, or happy. If you are in any difficulty tell me, and I will do all in my power to help you for her sake and your own."

These words struck the right chord in Warren Courtly, but he had not the courage to confess what he had done.

"I am upset over selling Holme Farm," he replied, "but there is nothing else, except the barefaced audacity of such a man as Felix Hoffman writing to Irene."

"You know the man?"

"Yes, and I told her he was a scoundrel. He shall feel my stick across his shoulders the next time we meet."

"Better to have no scenes," said the Squire. "Avoid him in the future, but give him to understand there must be no more letters written, or he will be handed over to the police."

"That will probably be the best way. I met him casually at Hurst Park, and he gave me some very good information."

"And on the strength of that," said the Squire, "I suppose he has stuck to you like a leech. I know these men, they ought to be ducked in a horsepond, they are pestilential nuisances, but unfortunately there is no way of killing them off."

Warren Courtly rode home, where another unpleasant

surprise awaited him. Irene had received a second letter from Felix Hoffman, returning the five pounds and thanking her for the loan.

"There," said Irene. "I am right, and the Squire is wrong. I felt sure from the tone of his letter he would return the money, so he cannot be quite so black as you painted him."

"I am very much surprised, I assure you," said Warren, "but the return of the money does not do away with the fact that it was a gross piece of impertinence on his part to write to you, and I shall call him to account for it."

This letter, returning the money, caused Warren Courtly much uneasiness. He knew it meant that Felix Hoffman was playing some clever game, and that trouble was brewing at no distant date. It was seldom Hoffman allowed a five-pound note to leave his possession, no matter how he obtained it. When he did so, it was generally with the certainty of getting many times its value in return.

CHAPTER IX

HOW ULICK BOUGHT THE SAINT

When Ulick Maynard returned to London after his brief visit to Eli Todd at Hazelwell, he went to his rooms in West Kensington. Here he had a comfortable flat, and lived as happily as possible under the circumstances. He missed his father's company; they were always together, and there had never been angry words between them until the night he left home. He sometimes wondered had he done right to leave Hazelwell in a sudden burst of anger, but he could not have remained under such a cloud of suspicion as his father enveloped him in.

If his father believed him guilty, what would the neighbours think? They would naturally one and all condemn him, so it was no doubt for the best he had gone away for a time.

London is the safest place in the world for a man to come to if he wishes to keep away from his friends and relations. It is a difficult matter to find anyone in the midst of the huge whirl of traffic and millions of people constantly pouring along its myriad thoroughfares.

Ulick avoided no one, nor did he shun any places he wished to visit, lest he might be recognised. He went about the same as any casual visitor to the city, and although he had been to London many times he had never become so well acquainted with it before.

At first time hung heavily on his hands. He missed all his country pursuits; the noise of the city jarred upon him, and he longed for the murmur of the stream, the sough of the wind amongst the trees, the rustle of the grass, the songs of birds, the lowing of cattle, the bleating of sheep and lambs, and, more than all, the merry neighing of the horses, and the joyous bark of Bersak. He felt cramped, cooped up, unable to breathe freely, and his whole being revolted at the scenes around him. For hours he roamed the vast city, watching the human wrecks, the flotsam and jetsam of mankind, being tossed about in the whirlpool of London life, and wondered what became of them all, where they housed at night, where they ended their days, how they died, and if any living soul mourned their departure.

Christmas came soon after his arrival in London. It was the most dismal one he ever spent, and he knew at Hazelwell there would be a corresponding gloom. His heart was hardened against his father then, and it was with some amount of equanimity that he thought the Squire also suffered alone and in silence. Christmas Eve he spent in the city, and watched the children returning home ladened with toys and a variety of parcels, their little arms clasped round their treasures, holding them tight, fearful lest some mishap should befall them. He saw the worn faces of hard-working parents glowing with pride and joy at the thought that out of their toil they had been able to save something for their little ones' pleasure. Late that night he saw sights that made him shudder, and as he passed woman after woman he was half afraid to look at them, so utterly abandoned were their faces.

As he crossed Trafalgar Square he heard a faint moan, and looking in the direction from whence it came he saw a tiny boy and girl huddled close together on a seat. It was a bitterly cold night, and London was clothed in a dirty, drizzling sleet. He crossed over to the children, and the boy, pulling the girl closer to him, looked at him with big, starving, staring eyes. He questioned them and found they had no home, no place wherein to lay their heads, and they meant to remain there for the night, unless the policeman moved them on, or took them away. He asked if they could find lodgings if he gave them the money, and the boy said he could, but looked incredulous at the prospect of such good fortune.

Ulick gave him ten shillings in silver, and when the lad saw it in his hand he cried for joy and roused his sister to look at the harvest. She inquired what the coins were, and he said shillings, and that they would last them for many days, until long after Christmas.

They showered thanks upon Ulick in their childish way, and then trudged across the Square with their arms round each other. They looked back as they reached the Strand, and he waved his hand to them. That night he slept badly, he wondered why there was so much misery in the world.

Time passed on, and early in the spring he commenced to think a little racing would be a pleasant recreation. He had no occasion to hide from his fellows, for he had done no wrong, and could hold his head high with the rest of them.

He went to Epsom and saw the City and Suburban, and while there he met his father's old trainer, Fred May, who was delighted to see him again. The Squire had not raced much during the past few years, generally selling his yearlings at Newmarket. Fred May had won him many good races, and trained Honeysuckle when she won her big event.

Ulick did not tell the trainer that he had left Hazelwell, he saw no necessity for it. They chatted about old times, and May made many inquiries about the Squire.

"Do you think he will ever race again?" asked May.

"I don't fancy he will, but I shall, and I should not mind speculating in something useful and handing it over to your care," replied Ulick.

"You really mean it?" said Fred May.

"Of course I do," laughed Ulick.

"Then I know where you can buy a youngster that will come out at the top of the tree, and if he is well-trained will make a grand three-year-old."

"A two-year-old now?" asked Ulick.

"Yes; he is by Father Confessor out of Hilda, and is known as the Saint. He has not run yet, but you can accept my word for it he is a flyer. He's at Epsom, at Lowland Lodge, and we can have a look at him after the races."

"Is the figure high? I do not wish to give a big price, and I would have rather bought a three or four-year-old," said Ulick.

"Buy the Saint if you can, you will never regret it," said the trainer.

After the races they walked down to Lowland Lodge and inspected the Saint.

"Why, he's a grey!" exclaimed Ulick, in a disappointed tone, as the door of the box was opened.

"And there's been many a good grey racehorse," replied Fred May. "Never mind the colour. Look him over, and fancy he is a bright bay, or brown, or a chestnut, or anything you like, only forget he's a grey, and then I'm sure you will not find a fault in him."

Ulick was no mean judge of blood horses, and, acting on the trainer's advice and ignoring the colour, he looked the Saint carefully over. He was rather anxious to find an excuse for declining to buy him, but he failed; he was unable to "fault" the colt in any way. He was well shaped all over. His legs were sound and clean, also his feet, well let down behind, tapering off like a greyhound; he had also a strong back and loins, and muscular thighs. There was plenty of him in front of the saddle, and his shoulders sloped well, his neck set on perfectly, and his head denoted courage and endurance. He seemed to be shaped for speed, and evidently possessed staying powers. His colour was not prepossessing, for he was not a good grey, and this was the only fault Ulick could find with him.

"Well!" exclaimed the trainer, with a smile, when he saw he had finished his inspection, "what do you think of him?"

"He is perfect in everything except his colour. I must say he is about as bad a colour as a racehorse well could be," replied Ulick.

"Granted that is so, his colour will not prevent him winning. Do you recollect Buchanan winning the Lincolnshire Handicap? No, of course not, what am I thinking of? You were a little chap then, I expect. Well, he was a funny looking grey, something after the style of the Saint, but he spread-eagled his field that day, and no mistake. The race was run in a snowstorm, and he faced it like a lion; it blew straight down the course, and it was no light thing for a horse to meet it in his teeth. He was a good grey, and I have known others; it is all prejudice, the colour is all right if the horse is good enough."

Ulick hesitated. He felt tempted to buy, for he knew Fred May's judgment was sound, and that he seldom made mistakes. He had not yet asked the price, perhaps it would be prohibitory—he almost hoped so.

The owner of the Saint was anxious to sell him for the same reason that Ulick hesitated about buying; he did not like his colour. On this account he asked a price that he thought would tempt a wavering purchaser.

Two hundred guineas was the price placed upon the Saint, and Ulick was forced to acknowledge it was reasonable. He had seen yearlings sold for five times the amount that had turned out utter failures, and here was a two-year-old that in all probability would make a clinker.

Fred May made no remark when he heard the price asked for the Saint, but he was determined if Ulick did not buy him he would.

"The figure is reasonable," said Ulick, "but I abominate the colour. That is the only reason I do not feel inclined to buy him."

"Then you will not have him?" asked the owner.

"No, thanks, and I am very much obliged to you for showing him me and placing him on offer," said Ulick.

The owner laughed, and said, "I am not surprised; I want to sell him because he is such a confoundedly bad colour."

"Have you quite made up your mind?" asked Fred May.

"Yes," replied Ulick.

"Then I'll take him at that figure," said Fred, much to their surprise. "I don't care twopence about his colour, there's the make and shape of a great horse there, and, grey or no grey, he'll win races."

"When will you take delivery?" asked the seller.

"He can return home with the horses I have at Epsom. They are at Tom Lucas's boxes. I'll send a lad round for him this evening," said May.

The bargain was completed; and Fred May invited Ulick to accompany him to the house where he was staying for the races.

Nothing more was said about the Saint until after dinner, when Fred May remarked that they might as well go and see if the ugly-coloured customer looked any better in his new box.

"I am afraid the change of boxes will not improve him," said Ulick, "but we can go and see."

The Saint was quite at home in his quarters, and the lad who brought him from Lowland Lodge said he was as quiet as an old sheep.

"That is another point in his favour," said May. "There will be no trouble with the starting machine in his case."

Ulick half wished he had bought him, more especially as the trainer seemed so satisfied with his bargain.

"Do you really think he will make a good horse?" asked Ulick, when they were in the house again.

"I am as certain of it as anyone can be over such ticklish things as racehorses. I never saw a much better shaped colt, and he's cheap enough at the price."

"I almost wish I had bought him," said Ulick.

"You can have him at the price I paid if you wish," said May.

"That would hardly be fair to you," replied Ulick. "I must give you something for your trouble. If you had not had the courage to buy him, despite his colour, I should not have the chance perhaps now."

"If you really want him, pay me the two hundred guineas for him, and let me train him," said May.

"That goes without saying," replied Ulick. "Of course, you will train him; I should not think of sending horses elsewhere."

"Then let us conclude the bargain."

"Very well. I will give you the two hundred guineas and leave him in your charge," replied Ulick, and in this way he became the owner of the Saint.

During the season the Saint fully endorsed the good opinion formed of him by Fred May. He won four races, in one of which he beat the best of his year, much to the delight of Ulick and the trainer.

The Saint went into winter quarters with an unbeaten record, and racing men thought it a pity he was not in any of the classical events, but they were determined to keep an eye upon him in handicaps.

Eli Todd was surprised when he learned that Mr. Lanark, the owner of the Saint, was none other than Ulick Maynard. The Squire would have been still more astounded had he been enlightened upon the subject.

It was Ulick's firm determination to find Janet Todd and induce her to return home. He was thoroughly tired of being away from Hazelwell, and he meant to force Janet, if necessary, to tell her father the truth, and then Eli could impart it to the Squire. He puzzled his brains to think what Eli meant by saying it would cause even more trouble than had already occurred if what he partly suspected turned out true.

Ulick, however, did not believe that Eli would withhold a confession from Janet from his father.

"He wants more than mere suspicion to act upon," said Ulick to himself, "and he shall have it if I can find Janet. I can deal with the man who allowed the blame to fall upon me when I discover his name, and I shall not spare him."

He often thought about Irene, and wondered how she and Warren Courtly got on together. He had never liked Warren, although he had nothing against him, except his constant attentions to Irene, and as a result his marriage with her. This, however, he knew was partially his own fault, although he doubted if he would ever have succeeded in winning her. He left the course clear for Warren, and therefore rendered it a comparatively easy task for him.

It never occurred to Ulick that Warren Courtly had anything to do with the disappearance of Janet Todd. Had it been suggested to him he would have laughed at the idea as absurd.

CHAPTER X

"THE CURIOSITY"

The Saint's first appearance as a three-year-old was at Kempton Park in the Pastures Handicap, a mile race on the Jubilee course. Having wintered well, as the trainer anticipated, he developed into a fine three-year-old, and in the early spring had a real good trial with some first-class handicap horses. Fred May was exceedingly anxious to place the colt well, and decided upon the Pastures Handicap because the distance was suitable, and the class of horses he was likely to meet in a five hundred pound race would not trouble him much.

Ulick agreed with him, and accordingly the Saint was entered.

Contrary to their expectations, there were some good horses in the race, including the winner of the Lincolnshire Handicap, and a four-year-old named Pinkerton, who had won the Jubilee Stakes the year before.

"We are in better company than I fancied we should be," said Fred May, when he glanced down the entries, "and I expect we shall get a biggish weight. We can strike him out if he is badly in."

The handicap, however, proved to be a good one, and although the Saint had eight stone, a big weight early in the year for a three-year-old, both Ulick and the trainer considered he had a chance. Pinkerton had eight stone twelve, and this horse they considered the most dangerous. There are few more enjoyable places than Kempton Park for racing in the spring, or, in fact, at any time of the year.

Although the Pastures Handicap was not the principal race of the day, it attracted the most attention, mainly on account of the Saint being a runner. His two-year-old performances placed him almost on a par with the Derby horses, and the favourite for that race would have been regarded as a certainty in the handicap with eight stone. It was generally acknowledged by the "clever division" that a four-year-old like Pinkerton ought to be able to give the Saint twelve pounds. Mulgar, Kit Cat, and Ringbell were also fair performers, and Kit Cat had been booked as a "rod in pickle" for some time past. As she had only seven stone, it was regarded as her "day out"—in other words, that the weight was right and she was going for the money.

The ring was kept busy when betting was opened on the Pastures Handicap. Four to one bar one, was first shouted, Pinkerton being the favourite, but these odds soon expanded until it was four to one on the field.

In the paddock the Saint was the great attraction. Everyone knew his two-year-old performances, and his remarkable colour always caused a mild sensation. He was "washy" enough as a two-year-old, but this spring he was almost white with a few "flea-bitten" spots on him.

"Looks as if he'd been powdered with black pepper and salt," was one characteristic remark, which certainly hit the mark.

Despite his colour, there was no mistaking the quality and fitness of the horse. He had been perfectly trained, hard and clean in his coat, no dandified polish on it, but a real glow of health.

"He'd make the Derby horses go if they ran against him now," said a well-known pressman.

"You are right, Harry. I fancy he'd start pretty near favourite. I think I shall back him," was the answer of a brother scribe.

The ladies crowded round "the curiosity," as the Saint was nicknamed, and a horse with a nickname is as popular as a rosy-cheeked schoolboy dubbed "apples." A nickname is a sure sign of something out of the common in man, boy, or horse.

"The curiosity" took the mobbing in good part, it troubled him not at all, although he condescendingly glanced round the ring from time to time, and, as Fred May saddled him, made playful snaps at his coat, and once succeeded in securing his hat.

Ben Sprig was to ride the Saint; a good jockey with a reputation for honesty. He was a miniature man, about thirty-five, capable of riding seven stone if necessary. His face was a study. Ben Sprig seldom smiled outwardly; he seemed to conceal all

72

expressions of joy inside his small frame, and the only signs of pleasure experienced were sundry chuckles that sounded like the cracking of nuts. He spoke jerkily, shooting out his words like darts, and taking time to consider between each one. His complexion was bronze, and his eyes were small and brown. He had beautifully-shaped small hands and feet, of which he was very proud. He was dapper in his dress, and always clean and spruce. His humour was proverbial, and as he always had a solemn countenance it proved the more effective. A man who laughs at his own jokes is like an advertiser who stares at his own advertisements. There was none of the advertising agent about Ben Sprig.

"Where's Ben?" asked May, as the bell rang.

"I'll hunt him up," said Ulick, as he hurried off towards the jockey's room.

Ben Sprig was a thorn in the side of all clerks of the course. They invariably had to hurry him up, and in nine cases out of ten he was always the last to leave the paddock. He had a habit of sneaking his mount up the course when the majority of the spectators thought all the horses were at the post.

"Come along, Ben," said Ulick. "I never saw such a fellow, you are always last."

"Leaving the paddock," said Ben, solemnly.

Ulick laughed as he replied, "Not always in that position at the finish, I grant you."

Ben was walking slowly along, the olive green jacket adopted by Ulick being almost hidden beneath a coat which came down to the heels of his boots.

Ulick was striding along in front; the clerk of the course gesticulating furiously at Ben, who took no notice whatever of him.

"Hurry up," he said, as he rode up to the jockey. "You're always last, I wonder you are not fined every time for being late at the post."

Ben pointed solemnly to the clock, and said—

"They are always behind time when you are clerk of the course."

73

Ben was quickly in the saddle, and rode the Saint quietly out on to the course, which was cleared of the crowd. He sidled up to the rails, and slipped along past the stands. He was almost rounding the bend before the people recognised the colours.

"I thought the Saint had gone down long ago?" said one.

"That's a trick of Ben Sprig's, he generally goes up last," was the reply.

The noise at Tattersall's was deafening, and although Pinkerton was a slight favourite, the money had poured in for Kit Cat to such an extent that she was about the worst runner in many of the books.

The Saint stood at six to one, and Ulick had succeeded in obtaining a point longer for his money.

There was no delay at the post, Mr. Coventry sending them off in his usual style.

Kit Cat was quickly on her legs, and came along at a great pace, the golden stars on the black jacket of her rider glittering in the sunlight. Mulgar's white jacket also showed prominently, and after a gap came Pinkerton, and the olive green on the Saint.

From the start the pace was fast, and Kit Cat was making the most of her light weight. She had an easy style of going, and looked strong enough to carry a couple of stone more. Her owner had not waited in vain to get in with seven stone, and the money proved the mare could go when required. He was regarded, not without reason, as a very smart man. His name, Conrad Rush, had often figured against large winning accounts in Monday's settlement, and the ring had a wholesale dread of him. He never did anything underhand, but he possessed an amount of patience that fairly wore the handicappers out.

The golden stars leading in a mile race meant mischief, and already backers of Kit Cat were on good terms with themselves. The mare rounded the bend going in grand style, revelling in her light weight, and pulling hard. So far, it was a one-horse race, but creeping up on the rails not far behind were Pinkerton's blue jacket, the Saint, and Mulgar. To these four horses it soon became evident the race belonged; which would win?

Already the murmur of many voices could be heard in the rings. The sound gradually increased until it swelled into a roar, and louder and louder it became as the horses drew nearer.

Kit Cat still held a commanding lead, and it seemed almost impossible she could be caught.

"They don't win there," said Fred May to Ulick, "and the Saint has a rare turn of speed."

"It's a lot of ground to make up," he replied, "but I hope he'll do it. Pinkerton is running well, but Kit Cat has such a light weight she ought to last it out."

"I fancy Conrad Rush has overshot his mark this time. I have never seen the mare cover a mile. She may do it, but I doubt it. Look at her now—by Jove, she's done, I felt pretty sure of it."

Ulick saw the rider on Kit Cat "niggling" at her, and a second or two later he raised his whip as he heard the horses behind drawing nearer.

The bookmakers were jubilant and howled with delight.

Kit Cat responded to the call, but it was a mere flash in the pan.

Pinkerton was the first to tackle her on the outside, and as he drew level she swerved towards him and bored him out. This left an opening on the rails, which looked dangerous to squeeze through. Ben Sprig never flinched when he got a chance, however small he took it. He did so on this occasion. He was watching the two horses in front of him with keen eyes, and no sooner did Kit Cat swerve than he slid the Saint forward with one great effort and secured the lead.

It was a clever bit of jockeyship on the part of the rider, a marvellous run on the part of the horse, and the combined effort drew forth a hearty cheer.

The rider of Pinkerton had not expected this; he fancied the Saint was shut in on the rails, and would have to go round him on the outside. When he saw the olive green jacket on the other side of Kit Cat, it is needless to say he was surprised.

Pinkerton was not beaten, and as the pair cleared Kit Cat a tremendous race home ensued. It was a thrilling moment. Pinkerton had won over this course, and that was in his favour. The Saint had not run on it before. The four-year-old and the three-year-old struggled gamely on, with a difference of twelve pounds between them.

Ulick was excited; he had not seen the Saint in such a tight place before, and he hoped he would get out of it.

The horses were close to the winning post, a few more strides would decide it. They fought out every yard of the ground. Ben Sprig was a great finisher. He graduated in a good school, and he clung to the old tradition that a bit left for a finish is worth a hundred yards at any other part of the race.

His face was set, and his little eyes gleamed. His small hands gripped the reins firmly, his knees pressed the Saint's sides, and he helped the horse all he knew how. The olive jacket and the blue were level, the next few strides would do it; which would win?

A moment of suspense, a second or two of breathless silence, then a mighty shout.

"The Saint! The Saint!"

Ulick echoed the cry.

"The Saint wins!" he shouted.

Ben Sprig's immovable face showed no signs of the triumph within. He knew he had ridden one of his best races, he felt much of the success was due to his horsemanship, and he was pleased with himself. He slid past the judge's box about three parts of a length in front of Pinkerton, with Kit Cat a bad third.

The Saint's performance was acknowledged on all sides to be a great one, and "the curiosity" was mobbed as Ben rode him in amidst cheers. Mr. Lanark was not well known, but the Saint had made the olive green jacket popular.

"You rode a splendid race, Ben," said Ulick. "I think the best you ever rode on him."

Ben Sprig had ridden the Saint throughout his two-year-old career.

"I agree with you," jerked Ben. "I did ride a good race, the saints be praised."

"I expect you felt a bit uneasy when you squeezed through on the rails?" laughed Ulick.

"Not at all; I'm used to squeezing. I've been squeezing all my life to make both ends meet," said Ben.

"Then from all accounts you have squeezed to some purpose," said Ulick, for Ben Sprig was reported to be rich.

"I could lend some of 'em a trifle, I have no doubt," he replied, "but look at the time I have been at it."

They joined Fred May in the paddock, and looked at the Saint walking round.

"He's the rummiest coloured beggar I ever rode or saw," said Ben.

"Bar his colour, what do you think of him?" asked May.

"He's an out-and-out good one, and as game as they make 'em. If it came to a match between him and the Derby winner I would back him, provided I rode him."

"That's a pretty tall order," said Ulick.

"It would come off, you can take my word for it," he replied.

A friend came up to Ulick, and they walked away together. After some conversation as to the merits of the Saint's victory, he said—

"How are you going back to town—by train?"

"Yes," replied Ulick.

"I have to go on to Windsor. Drive with me to Feltham and go to Waterloo from there, unless you will come with me?"

Ulick thanked him, said he would drive to Feltham, but declined to go to Windsor.

After the races they took a carriage to Feltham, driving through Hanworth Park, and down the High Street.

They were chatting over racing matters, when his friend exclaimed—

"By Jove! there's a pretty girl—well dressed, too."

Ulick looked up and gave a start of surprise.

It was Janet Todd. She had not seen him, of that he felt sure. She was going down the street, and he resolved to leave his friend at the station, walk back, and meet her. It was a lucky chance that caused him to come this way back from the races.

"Do you know her?" asked his friend, smiling, as he saw him start.

"I fancy I do; I am almost sure of it. I think I'll walk back and meet her after I leave you," he replied.

"I don't blame you, my friend," he said, laughing. "Does she come from your part of the world?"

"I am almost sure of it," replied Ulick; "at any rate, I mean to find out."

"Good luck to you," laughed his friend, as he shook hands and went into the station.

CHAPTER XI

FOR A WOMAN'S SAKE

Ulick walked out of the station yard and along the High Street. He saw Janet coming down on the opposite side of the road, and wondered whether it would be best to stop her or to watch where she went. He would, no doubt, surprise her if he spoke to her in the street, and perhaps the suddenness of his appearance might cause a scene. He decided it would be the better plan to allow her to pass, and then follow her. He went into a shop, made a trifling purchase, and saw her pass by.

When he went out she was turning round by the church, and he followed some distance away. He saw her enter a house, where she probably lived, but he waited some time in case she came out again. When she did not he went up to the door and rang the bell.

As he heard it ring he wondered who to ask for. She would not be living there under her own name, at all events it was unlikely.

Fortune favoured him, for Mrs. Hoffman was out and Janet was alone in the house.

She opened the door and stood face to face with Ulick.

The shock was great; she felt faint and giddy, and caught hold of the door, but, recovering herself, gasped out—

"Mr. Maynard, what are you doing here? How did you find me out?"

"I saw you as I drove from Kempton Park to Feltham, and came back from the station to meet you. I thought, however, it would be better to see you in your house, as I might have startled you in the street."

"I am very glad you did," she replied. "Will you come in?"

"Thank you, I should like to have a little conversation with you," he replied.

"I wonder if he knows?" thought Janet, and quickly decided he could hardly do so. Then arose the question should she tell him? No, it would be better to keep her secret for the present.

"You will not be offended if I put some plain questions to you, I hope," said Ulick. "I have suffered a good deal on your account; that must be my excuse."

"Ask me anything you like, and I will try and answer it," she replied.

"Are you living alone here?" he said.

"Yes," replied Janet. "Mrs. Hoffman and her son are the only other occupants of the house."

"I am glad of it," he replied; "it will make my task less difficult."

"What do you wish to do?" she asked, timidly.

"I saw your father early in the New Year, on New Year's Day, and I promised him I would find you, and persuade you to return home," he replied.

"I cannot do that," said Janet, firmly. "It is impossible. You would be the first to say so, if you knew all."

"Tell me all, and let me judge what is best to be done," he replied.

"That, also, is impossible, I know you mean well, and I thank you for your kindness."

"Your father will be very glad to have you back; he will forget the past; he has long since forgiven you, but not the man who tempted you to leave home. I wish I had known what you were about to do the night I left home. I would have stopped you and saved you at any cost."

Janet Todd shuddered. She was glad he had not met her and Warren Courtly, or there was no telling what might have happened.

"I cannot undo all I have done," she said. "Some day it may be possible for me to go back to my father without any danger or trouble to others, but at present I cannot. Believe me, I would do so if it were possible."

"Consider well what you are saying," he said. "If I give your father your address he will come and take you away, you cannot refuse to go with him."

"You must not do it—indeed you must not," pleaded Janet, earnestly. "Oh, if you only knew, you would leave the house at once. It is better for you to go and forget you have seen me." He was surprised at her agitation, which he saw was genuine. There was something in the background he could not understand, and her father had thrown out hints in the same way. What was the mystery, and why was it necessary to keep him in the dark?

"Janet, will you tell me who the man is you ran away with? I will not mention it to anyone if you desire me not to do so. If I know, I may be better able to help you," said Ulick.

"I cannot tell you; it is impossible," she replied. "Please do not ask me?"

"It must have been someone in the neighbourhood, but I cannot think who would do such a cowardly action," he said.

This was dangerous ground, and Janet said quickly—

"You can tell my father you have seen me, that I am well, and will come to him as soon as I possibly can."

"That is not sufficient. It is my duty to let him know where you are."

"If you do I must leave here, and I am very comfortable. Mrs. Hoffman is kind to me, and has always been so. Please allow matters to remain as they are."

Ulick looked at her, and thought his friend was right in describing Janet as a pretty woman. She evidently lived a regular life, and he was glad to see a healthy glow on her cheeks. Whatever her faults in the past, she was living a decent, quiet life now, of that he felt certain. It would be a great consolation to Eli to know this.

"If you feel compelled to remain hidden here for a time," he said at last, "I will keep your secret, but you must allow me to write to your father and tell him you are well and living a respectable life. That will ease his mind, and he will wait for your return more patiently. It is right he should know, for he has suffered much on your account."

She thanked him, and gave the permission he required, again entreating him not to mention her address.

The gate opened, and Mrs. Hoffman came into the house. She was surprised to see Ulick, and looked at him sharply, thinking to herself, "I wonder what he is doing here? Perhaps he is a friend of Mr. Warren's?"

Mrs. Hoffman always addressed Janet as Mrs. Warren; it sounded more respectable.

Janet was at a loss what to say; she did not wish to give Ulick's name, in case Warren Courtly might hear he had called.

"A friend of yours, Mrs. Warren?" said Mrs. Hoffman, with a smile.

"Yes," said Janet, "a very old friend. I knew him when I was a little girl."

"Mrs. Warren," thought Ulick, thinking the name sounded familiar, but never dreaming of connecting it with Warren Courtly.

Mrs. Hoffman was fond of hearing herself talk, and launched out upon a variety of topics until Ulick wished her anywhere but in his presence. He thought, however, it was diplomatic, for Janet's sake, to be polite, and Mrs. Hoffman was delighted to find such an attentive listener. As a rule, her tirades were cut short with scant ceremony.

She pressed him to have a cup of tea, and, thinking this was the only way to get rid of her for a time he consented.

He went to the window and looked out into the street and saw someone walking down. He could hardly believe his eyes when he recognised Warren Courtly.

"What on earth is he doing here?" he thought.

Janet followed him, and when she saw Warren she turned as pale as death, standing almost rigid, unable to move.

They must not meet. Whatever happened they must not meet. That was her one thought, her sole desire.

Ulick's eyes were fixed upon Warren. She pulled his sleeve. When he turned round and saw her face it told him all.

"Good God," he exclaimed. "Irene, what about Irene?"

He seized Janet's wrist, and pressed it so tightly that she almost screamed out with pain.

"Irene, his wife; good heavens, his wife, she must never know! Do you hear, she must never know; it would kill her. Do you hear me?"

"Yes," said Janet.

"Promise you will never breathe a word to her of this."

"I promise. You will help me if I require help?"

"I will, Janet. He must not see me," he said.

Janet pulled him towards the door and led him into the kitchen.

"Well, I never!" exclaimed Mrs. Hoffman.

"There is no time for any explanation," said Ulick. "Mr. ——"

"Mr. Warren is coming," put in Janet, "and Mr. Hazelwell"—it was the name that came first to her mind—"does not wish to meet him; they are not friends."

The door bell rang.

"Keep him here until Mr. Warren is gone," said Janet. "I will attend to the door."

Mrs. Hoffman was shocked. Why was it necessary for Mr. Hazelwell's visit to be concealed from Mr. Warren? She would not allow these goings on in her house. One thing, however, there was no getting over, and that was there was a gentleman in her kitchen, and she had asked him to have some tea. He was a good-looking gentleman into the bargain, and Mrs. Hoffman flattered herself there were considerable remains of her early beauty left.

"I am sorry this has occurred," said Ulick; "but I really do not wish to meet Mr. Warren."

"Didn't you know it was Mrs. Warren who lived here?" she asked.

"No, I saw her in Feltham. She was a playmate of mine years ago. I had no idea she was married."

"It is strange you should know Mr. Warren, too," said Mrs. Hoffman, curiously.

"Remarkable, I call it," he replied, as he accepted the cup of tea handed him.

He heard voices in the next room and the tones were angry.

Ulick was dumbfounded at the discovery he had made. He saw now, and understood Janet's reason for not wishing to return home, and he appreciated her delicacy. It was some consolation to think Warren Courtly got into this mess before he married Irene, not after; and yet, judging from his presence here, he was keeping up the connection. His feelings can be better imagined than described. He loved Irene, he had found out the truth ever since he lost her. She must never know it was Warren Courtly who tempted Janet away from her home and allowed all the suspicion to fall upon himself. At the thought of Warren's perfidy, his blood boiled, and he would have gone into the next room with pleasure and called him to account, There was no reason why he should not do so. No reason? Only one, and that everything to him. He could bear the blame cast unjustly upon himself, the separation from his father, the loss of all the pursuits he loved, and a hundred times more, for Irene's sake. Irene was the one reason why he would not call Warren Courtly to account. He knew her nature, and how she would suffer if the truth reached her ears. She was not likely to hear it from anyone except himself or Janet, and she had promised not to tell. Did Eli suspect Warren Courtly? He thought of his words, and felt he meant that if what he suspected turned out true, it would cause great trouble at Anselm Manor. Eli would not be the man to cause that trouble.

The voices in the next room grew louder, and Mrs. Hoffman

said, "I am afraid they are quarrelling. Mr. Warren is a very irritable man."

"Does he come here often?" asked Ulick.

"No, he leaves her too much alone. He ought to be thankful he has me to look after her. Mrs. Warren is young, pretty, and inexperienced; he has no business to neglect her."

Ulick was glad to hear he neglected her; it was a sign he wished to spare Irene's feelings.

Warren remained about half an hour, and then left. He would have been very uneasy had he known Ulick Maynard was on the premises, and still more that he knew all about his connection with Janet. He had, as usual, quarrelled with her over money matters, but she had won in the end, as she was bound to do, considering the hold she had over him. She did not mean to let him shirk his responsibilities and he had no idea she would not have betrayed him to Irene under any circumstances.

She came into the kitchen and said, "You may come in now, Mr. Hazelwell—the coast is clear."

Ulick was glad to escape from Mrs. Hoffman, and when she was left alone that good lady commenced to sum up the situation to her own satisfaction.

"They are rivals, that's what it is," she said; "and this one is worth half-a-dozen Mr. Warrens. There's no telling what men will do where a pretty face is concerned. I know what it is myself, and to think I should have thrown myself away on such a fellow as Hoffman when I might have had anybody in those days. Mrs. Warren's in my charge, and she must be careful; but I like a little bit of romancing, and it strikes me I'm likely to get it in this situation."

Ulick had a serious talk with Janet.

"Is it because Warren Courtly is the man who took you away from home that you decline to return to your father's house?" he asked.

"Yes."

"I think you are right, now I know the facts. It will be better for me not to mention having seen you; it will only make Eli uneasy and anxious to know more."

She agreed with him, and promised to write to him if necessary.

"Were you quarrelling?" he added.

"We had some words, as usual, about money matters."

"He makes you an allowance still?"

"Yes, I could not live here without, and he has a right to do it," she replied.

"Mrs. Hoffman says he seldom comes here?"

"That is true."

"I am glad," said Ulick.

"So am I. When he married Miss Carstone I made up my mind to see as little of him as possible. He promised to marry me when I ran off with him," said Janet.

"He deceived you, and deserves to suffer for it, but his wife must not be dragged into it," he said.

"She will never learn anything from me," Janet answered, earnestly.

Ulick went back to London thinking over the varied chances of the day, and wondering at the strange discovery he had made.

So it was Warren Courtly who had robbed Eli of his daughter, and allowed the blame to rest on him. He would let Warren see that he knew the truth, that much satisfaction he meant having, but Irene must be shielded no matter what happened. How different events might have turned out had he stuck to his guns and won Irene, in spite of Warren Courtly, and the suspicions surrounding himself. Had he done so, no doubt the truth would have come to light in a very short time; as it was, he must trust to his luck to clear the way for him.

CHAPTER XII

TWO SCHEMERS

The Squire noticed an estrangement had taken place between Irene and her husband. She was too proud to allow her real feelings to appear on the surface, but he saw below it and knew there was discord somewhere.

Redmond Maynard, since his son's departure, had led a lonely life. Everyone in the county sympathised deeply with him, but he was not a man to be soothed with kindly words; on the contrary, they irritated him. He went about his daily avocations as usual, but it was evident he had lost much of the interest in his surroundings. Dr. Harding ordered a change, but the Squire protested he was in a perfect state of health, and that there was no occasion for him to leave Hazelwell. The doctor was an old and valued friend, in addition to being his medical attendant. He practised in various parts of the county, his connection being select and extensive. Dr. Harding's was a familiar figure in the hunting field, and when he could spare the time he was nothing loth to attend a race meeting. He was an excellent shot, and always had a standing invitation to join the parties at Hazelwell. Of late, however, visitors there had been few and far between, and Dr. Harding saw the Squire was gradually falling into a fit of despondency which boded ill for his health. He spoke to Irene about it, knowing the influence she had over him, and requested her to persuade him to go south for a time. This she did in her own winning way, promising Warren and herself would accompany him if he thought well.

"That is an inducement certainly, to have your company," he said. "I will think it over. I expect Harding has been putting you up to this," he added, smiling.

"Dr. Harding is only anxious about your health, and I am sure he advises you for the best," she said.

"I am aware of that," replied the Squire; "but we do not always follow the advice we ask. It is foolish, of course, and we ought to obey the doctor when we call him in. I rather fancy a change would do you good, Irene, you are not happy."

She looked troubled and said quickly—

"You are mistaken, I am perfectly happy; I have everything to make me contented."

"Has Warren been behaving himself lately?" he asked.

"He always behaves himself," was her answer.

"I am glad you think so; I do not," he said gruffly. "Warren is going the pace, and you know it."

His anxiety about Irene caused him for a time to forget his own troubles.

Eli Todd watched the Squire, and noted how worn and aged he was growing. This caused him many qualms of conscience; he knew the cause, and would have liked to remove it. He wrote a long letter to Ulick, telling him how his father's health suffered, and begging him to return. This caused him to wonder if he was doing right in remaining away. Now that he knew everything connected with Janet's disappearance from home, he felt it was impossible for him to go to Hazelwell and meet Irene, as he was sure to do. He wrote to Eli, explaining as well as he could that it was impossible for him to return at present, but circumstances might arise which would enable him to do so at no distant date. With this Eli had to rest contented, but he would have preferred something more definite.

It was shortly after the Saint's great race with Pinkerton at Kempton that the Squire came into Eli's cottage and sat down for a chat. Eli gave him full particulars of all the mares and youngsters in the stud, and said there would be some good prices realised at Doncaster in September.

"Honeysuckle's foal will be a tip-topper," said Eli. "He'll run well into four figures."

"I shall not sell him," replied the Squire.

Eli was glad to hear this; it meant the Squire thought of racing again.

"Shall you have him trained?" he asked.

"Yes, it is some time since I gave Fred May a turn. By the way, he has got hold of a champion in the Saint. That must have been a splendid race at Kempton. I wonder who Mr. Lanark is?"

"A new recruit to the turf," said Eli, smiling, "and he has made a rare good start." "He little thinks his son owns the Saint," thought Eli.

"He has got into the right hands. Fred May is thoroughly honest. Mr. Lanark, whoever he is, may congratulate himself. I wonder if he would sell the Saint?" said the Squire, half to himself.

Eli smiled; he thought it would be a curious thing if the Squire bought his son's horse. It occurred to him this might be the means of bringing them together.

"I should think it would be a difficult matter to induce him to part with him," said Eli.

"There can be no harm in trying," said the Squire. "I like the Saint's breeding; he would do well for the stud."

"Why not run down to Fred May's and see what can be done?" said Eli. "It will be a change for you."

"I think it will, and you had better come with me. I ought to write and let him know we are coming."

"I will do it to save you the trouble," said Eli.

"Very well, fix it for next Thursday, if that will suit Mr. Lanark, providing he is willing to sell," replied the Squire.

Eli cudgelled his brains how to bring about the meeting he desired. If Ulick knew his father was coming to Newmarket to see the Saint he would not be present, of that Eli felt certain. The only plan that suggested itself to him was to take Fred May into his confidence, for it was evident to Eli the trainer knew nothing of the misunderstanding between father and son. He wrote his letter after much deliberation, and anxiously awaited the reply. It came by return of post, and in it the trainer plainly showed how astonished he was at the breach between them.

"I will do all in my power to help you to heal it," he wrote, "but

I am afraid we shall get into trouble. Neither the Squire nor his son like being dictated to, and they will probably think we have taken a liberty. However, we will risk it. Bring him on Thursday, and I'll see that his son is here, you can leave that to me. If we can effect a reconciliation we shall have done much good. The Saint is an extraordinarily good colt, equal to the best Derby form, and I am very glad I advised Mr. Maynard to buy him. Tell the Squire there is no price upon him, but that Mr. Lanark will be delighted to see him and show him his champion, and one or two more he has in my stable."

Eli sent a note up to the Squire stating the matter was arranged, and they had better go to London on the Wednesday, and on to Newmarket next day.

To this arrangement he agreed, and sent Bob Heather with a letter to tell Irene of his intention.

"If you and Warren come to town I will meet you at the Walton Hotel on Friday."

Irene sent back a reply to the effect that they would be there, as Warren had to go up to town again at the end of the week.

When Ulick received a letter from his trainer requesting him to go to Newmarket on Wednesday, he hastened down at once, fearing something might have gone wrong with the Saint.

"He's all right," said Fred May, in reply to Ulick's anxious inquiries, "but I have some rather startling news for you. A gentleman is coming to see him to-morrow; he wishes to buy him. I thought you would have no objection to showing him the Saint yourself."

Ulick laughed as he replied, "He is coming on a useless errand; I would not sell him at any price."

"Never refuse a good offer," said Fred May.

"Surely you would not like to lose him?" he replied.

"Certainly not, but I should advise you all the same to take a stiff price."

"Don't you think he will stand training?"

"Not a shadow of doubt about that," was the trainer's reply.

"Then I shall not part with him. Who is the gentleman?"

"I am not quite sure, but I fancy he is rather an exalted person," said Fred, mysteriously.

"You have brought me down on a wild-goose chase," laughed Ulick. "You don't even know the name of the intending purchaser. I am surprised at you, Fred; however, I forgive you. I am always glad of an excuse to run down to Newmarket and have a gallop on the Heath."

The Squire and Eli came by an early train, and arrived at Stanton House, the trainer's residence, unseen by Ulick, who happened to be reading the paper in Fred May's room.

After a few words of welcome with his old patron, the trainer said he would tell Mr. Lanark they were here, and left the room. Eli felt very uncomfortable; he wondered if there would be an explosion. He had agreed with Fred May that it would be better to leave them alone together.

The door opened, and the trainer said, "This is Mr. Lanark, I think you know him?"

Father and son were face to face, and, taking advantage of their astonishment and consternation, the trainer and Eli beat a retreat, wondering how their plot would succeed.

For a few moments neither of them spoke. Both knew they had been brought together by Eli and the trainer. At last a smile came over the Squire's face, and he said, as he held out his hand, "We have been caught cleverly, Ulick, and I trust it is all for the best; it is a long time since we met, my boy." His voice shook at the finish, and this touched Ulick; he noticed how his father had changed, he seemed much older, and his face more worn. He clasped his hand and said—

"We have both suffered; it was all a mistake." He seemed at a loss for words. Had his father decided to do him justice, or did he still suspect him? It would be impossible for him to return to Hazelwell at present, and be constantly meeting Warren and his wife; that was more than he could endure, and yet he was unable to explain the reason to his father.

91

"So you are Mr. Lanark," said the Squire, laughing more heartily than he had done for many a day.

Eli and the trainer, listening like two guilty schoolboys in the hall, heard him, and the former said, joyfully—

"It's all right, Fred, that's the Squire's laugh, and right glad I am to hear it."

"It's splendid," said Fred, as he rubbed his hands in high glee; "we must crack a bottle over this, Eli, come along."

"I am Mr. Lanark," said Ulick, "and I own the Saint, but he is not for sale," he added, smiling.

"Never mind the horse at present; tell me what you have been doing," said the Squire.

"Living quietly in a flat in West Kensington, and doing a little racing," replied Ulick.

"Not quite so pleasant as Hazelwell?" inquired his father.

"There is no place quite like Hazelwell to my mind," said his son. "I was fearfully dull and miserable at first, but I have become fairly used to it now."

"You will come back to our home?" was the next question.

Ulick looked troubled; what could he say, how make an excuse?

"There is no occasion to hesitate," said the Squire. "Return with me to-day; the flat can look after itself."

The temptation was great. He thought of Hazelwell and all it meant to him; then he thought of Irene. If he was constantly in Warren's company he felt he must betray himself. Better to stay away, far better for all of them.

"I cannot return to-day, father," he said, quietly. "I have very good reasons for not doing so. Trust me, believe in me; I am acting for the best, as one day you will discover."

The Squire's face clouded. "He dare not face us all after what he has done," was his thought. He sighed heavily, and his son knew what it meant.

"You still believe me guilty," he said. "You are wrong, quite wrong. I can prove my innocence, but you ought not to require that of me. Cannot you trust me, father?"

The appealing tone in his voice was unmistakable, there was a ring of sincerity in it, and the Squire wavered. Ulick had not been accustomed to deceiving him. If he could only bring himself to believe in his innocence; but the evidence was damning, and now his refusal to return to Hazelwell confirmed it.

"Do you know who took Janet Todd away from home?" he asked.

"Yes," replied Ulick, in a low voice.

"Ah!" exclaimed the Squire, in a tone of satisfaction. "Then why have you not given me his name long ago?"

"Because I only discovered it the other day, and that quite by accident."

"Who is the scoundrel?"

"I cannot tell you."

"You must," thundered the Squire.

Ulick remained silent, nothing his father might say would make him break his resolve. It was hard, very hard, and at that moment he hated Warren Courtly heartily.

"Come, my boy," said his father, in a milder tone, "let there be no more differences between us. Are you satisfied if I say I am convinced of your innocence, and ask you to forgive me for my unjust suspicions? I regret the hasty, angry words I said that night. Come back home with me, and let bygones be bygones."

Ulick was moved, for he knew what it cost his father to speak such words, and acknowledge himself in the wrong. It was an appeal that cut him to the heart to refuse.

"If you knew all, father, you would say I was acting right not to return home at present. To hear you say you are convinced of my innocence has lifted a heavy load from me, and I thank you for those words with all my heart. How I long to return to Hazelwell, you must know, and therefore will understand the weighty reasons I have for not doing so. Trust me, father, believe in me, and I shall be the happiest man alive."

The Squire did not hesitate. He spoke steadily as he said, "I will trust you, my son. We have been separated too long. If you cannot return with me, I know there must be grave cause of which I know nothing. What it is I cannot imagine, but you will tell me some day, and I hope and pray that it will not be long. If you will not return with me to Hazelwell, you must come to the Walton with me and spend a few days."

"Willingly," said Ulick. "It will be like the good old times for us to be together again."

"I feel a new man," said the Squire, heartily, as he rose to his feet. "We will go and find those two schemers, Eli and Fred, and then have a look at the Saint."

CHAPTER XIII

THE SQUIRE AND THE SAINT

Redmond Maynard opened the door, and, followed by his son, went in search of the culprits. He knew his way about Stanton House, having often stayed there when Fred May trained his horses.

"I know where we shall find them," he said, "in May's room." They entered without ceremony and surprised the worthy pair enjoying a glass of champagne. They looked ludicrously guilty, and the Squire burst out laughing.

"You think you are very clever, no doubt," he said. "As it happens, everything has turned out for the best, but you might have got into trouble had it been otherwise."

"We had not much doubt about succeeding, or we should not have risked it," said Eli. "I am sure you are not sorry we did so."

"No, we are perfectly satisfied," replied the Squire, "and you both deserve credit for all you have done."

The trainer sent for another bottle of champagne, and the Squire and Ulick joined them.

"There is no chance of buying the Saint, Mr. Lanark says," remarked the Squire, smiling; "but as the horse is in the family I do not see that it matters much. One thing you must promise me, when he has finished racing you will send him to the Hazelwell stud."

"With pleasure," replied his son. "But he will stand a lot of training."

"I shall be surprised if he is not running as an aged horse," said the trainer, "for I never saw one with better legs or a sounder constitution; he is built for work, and cannot have too much of it. I only wish he was in the Derby, he is the very horse for that race."

"Let us go and see him," said the Squire. And they went towards the stables.

"I wonder what my father will think of his colour?" said Ulick to the trainer.

"It will surprise him, and he will be disappointed as you were, until he looks him over," was the reply.

"Eli, I shall not forget what you have done for us," said the Squire, as they walked across the yard. "I know it was your plan that brought us together. What made you think of it?"

"I saw you were feeling the separation more every week, and I determined to put a stop to it if I could, so I took Fred May into my confidence, and he eagerly agreed to my scheme."

"I wonder why Ulick will not return to Hazelwell with me?" mused the Squire.

"Is he not going home with you?" asked Eli, surprised.

"No, he says he has good reasons for not doing so. He knows who ran away with Janet, but he cannot tell me. Do you know?" asked the Squire, quickly.

"No," stammered Eli, thinking to himself perhaps Ulick's suspicions rested upon the same man as his own.

The Squire looked at him keenly, and said, "I believe you do. Confound it, I cannot make it out at all; why am I kept in the dark?"

Eli was glad when the trainer called out, "You are going too far; this is the Saint's box."

The Squire's mind was diverted, and he turned sharply round and walked back.

The trainer threw open the door of the box, and the Saint was stripped for their inspection.

The Squire looked at him in astonishment, and said, "Is this a joke, that cannot be the Saint? What a horrible colour! I never saw such a dirty grey before."

They laughed, and Eli was as much taken aback as his master.

96

"That is the Saint," said Ulick, "and I am not surprised you do not like his colour. I thought as you think when I first looked at him, and so did his owner, who parted with him solely because of his colour, and has regretted it ever since. I refused to purchase him for no other reason."

"Then who bought him?" asked the Squire.

"Fred May, and resold him to me at the price he gave for him. If it had not been for him I should not have had the colt at all."

"Upon my word I cannot help being disappointed," said the Squire. "He is not fit to look at."

The trainer laughed heartily, as he replied, "Come, Mr. Maynard, that is too bad, after all he has done. He has never been beaten yet, and do not forget he 'downed' the present Derby favourite as a two-year-old. Forget his colour, and examine him for his good qualities. I do not think you will find a fault with him."

The Squire went up to the Saint and carefully handled him. He was a considerable time making his inspection, and said at the conclusion—

"You are right; I cannot find fault with him, he is perfect, except for his colour. What a pity it is; it will never do to breed from him."

"I should chance it," said Ulick. "He may get them a much better colour than himself, and as far as make and shape and performances are concerned, he cannot very well be beaten."

"When does he run again?" asked the Squire.

"In the Coronation Cup in Derby week. It is run over the Derby course, and we want to show them what he can do. He'll meet last year's Derby winner, the Cesarewitch winner, and the Gold Cup winner of last season; if that is not a test of his quality, I do not know where it is to be found," said May.

"That will be a race," replied the Squire, "and I must be there to see it. I have a very good colt foal out of old Honeysuckle I am going to keep, and I shall send him to you at the back-end."

"I shall be very pleased to have him," replied May. "What a

wonder Honeysuckle was on the turf, and at the stud she has been even a greater success."

"And that does not always follow," said the Squire.

"By no means," replied the trainer. "The contrary is often the case."

The other horses at Stanton House were looked over, and after luncheon the Squire and his son returned to London, Eli going back to Hazelwell by a different route.

On their way up to town Ulick gave his father a full account of his doings since he left home; and the Squire, in return, informed him of the course of events at Hazelwell.

"If it had not been for Irene I should have been still more lonely," he said. "She was with me last winter for some time, and cheered me up, although I am rather afraid she was not particularly happy herself. I wish you had fallen in love with her instead of Warren, it would have been a good thing for all of us."

"If he only knew how I loved her," thought Ulick. Aloud he said, "She ought to be happy. Anselm Manor is a fine place, and her husband has plenty of money."

"He had," remarked the Squire, "but I do not know whether it is the case now. He gambles and is seldom at home. He had to sell Holme Farm to pay his debts, it was the best part of the estate. He had not the sense to offer it to me; I would have given him half as much again as he sold it for."

Ulick was surprised to hear this; he knew Warren Courtly was very well off, and his gambling transactions must have been very heavy to force him to sell Holme Farm.

"Does Irene know of this?" he asked.

"Yes, she cannot be kept in the dark. They have not been married long, as you are aware, and yet I am very much afraid she has found out her mistake, and, what is worse, I encouraged her to accept him. It has all been a deplorable bungle, but I hope Warren will pull up in time."

They drove from Liverpool Street to the Walton Hotel, and Ulick sent round to his rooms for his clothes.

As he dressed for dinner he little thought that Warren Courtly and Irene were to be of the party; he was unaware of their presence in the hotel, his father purposely not having mentioned it in case it might drive him away.

It wanted half an hour to dinner-time, and he opened the window and looked out across the gardens, the Embankment, and the river. The scene attracted him, although he had seen it many times before; but the dull, dark beauty of the Thames, as it flows through the great city to the sea, possesses an irresistible fascination which seldom palls. London and the Thames are bound together by historical ties which can never be undone. The great watery highway glides heavily along under many vast bridges, past huge warehouses, docks, and shipping from all parts of the world, until it gradually empties itself into the Channel, and is lost in the vast sea. Ulick knew Paris well, and wondered why there were no steamers plying along the Thames as they did on the Seine. He thought it a shame this great river should be thus neglected, for no more imposing view of London can be obtained than from a boat.

He carelessly watched the traffic on the Embankment, and the people lounging on the seats in the gardens below. London is always busy, and yet it contains myriads of human beings whose sole occupation is to kill time.

At the dinner-hour he went downstairs. His father informed him he had engaged a table, and the waiter pointed it out to him. He crossed over and sat down. In a few minutes he saw his father enter the room, and almost fell off his chair in astonishment and dismay as he saw Warren Courtly and Irene with him.

"It is a little surprise I have not exactly prepared for you, but am giving you," said the Squire, smiling. "I have explained to them that we are quite reconciled, and that there are no differences between us."

Ulick shook hands mechanically with Warren Courtly, who felt very uneasy, and Irene, who did not conceal the pleasure it gave her to see him again.

"It is the best news I have heard since you left Hazelwell," she said. "I thought it too good to be true when your father told me of your meeting and reconciliation at Newmarket."

"And I am more than pleased to see you again," he said,

earnestly. "You have not quite forgotten your old playmate and companion?"

"Oh, no; I never can forget those days; they were the happiest of my life."

She did not think what she was saying until Warren said abruptly—

"That is not very complimentary to me."

Irene coloured slightly as she replied—

"You understand what I mean."

"And heard what you said," he replied.

"I am very glad Irene was so happy at Hazelwell," said the Squire. "We always tried to make her so."

The conversation during dinner-time seemed to drag; there was a feeling of restraint between the three younger members of the party which the Squire, who was overflowing with good-humoured happiness, failed to notice. He talked freely and well, and Ulick was glad of it. From time to time he glanced at Warren and thought—

"If he knew I had met Janet, and seen him in Mrs. Hoffman's house at Feltham, I wonder what he would do? He knows he has done me an irreparable injury, and yet it does not seem to trouble him much."

After dinner Warren Courtly said he had letters to write, and asked to be excused for half an hour.

The Squire went into the reading-room, "Just for a quiet doze," he said, smiling, and Irene and Ulick were left alone. They went on to the balcony and sat down. It was a beautiful May evening, much warmer than usual, and the air was refreshing after the heat of the room.

"You cannot know how the Squire has suffered during your absence," she said, after a few remarks on various topics. "Do you not think he is older, I mean has aged very much?"

"Yes," replied Ulick, "and I am very sorry if I have been the cause. Still, I could not have acted otherwise. I would do it again if necessary."

She wished to ask him if his father believed in him, knew he had accused him unjustly, but it was a delicate matter. Still, they were old friends, and there could be no harm in it.

"Is the Squire satisfied he made a mistake, and he was in the wrong?" she asked.

"Yes, I have that satisfaction, although I cannot return to Hazelwell at present."

"Not return!" she exclaimed, in surprise. "What reason can there possibly be for that?"

"A grave reason which I cannot explain to you, but which my father accepts, although he fails to understand; may I ask you to do the same?"

"Indeed, yes; but I am very, very sorry you are not coming home," she said.

"I am glad to hear you say that," he replied, earnestly, "because I value your good opinion very much, almost as much, if not quite, as my father's."

"You have always had my good opinion," she said, softly.

"Then you never believed me guilty?" he asked, eagerly.

She hesitated; she had at one time thought he might have become entangled with Janet. She would not deny it now.

"You must forgive me, Ulick," she said. "Remember, I heard the story from the Squire, and I had no opportunity of hearing your side. What else could I do? I confess I thought as he thought, but I no longer do so now you are reconciled."

"You thought me capable of stealing Janet Todd from her father, from Eli, who would have willingly done anything for me?" he said, reproachfully.

"Not that; no, not that," she replied. "I never gave that a thought."

"You did not believe Janet went away with me?"

"No, I was sure she did not."

He looked surprised, she spoke so certainly.

"Why were you sure?"

"Because Eli told me you left the house alone, when Janet was in her room."

"How did he know, he left us alone together when he went out?"

"He was sure of it, and I believed what he told me," she said.

Ulick thought Eli must know more about Janet's disappearance than he cared to tell. He did not know where she was, but it was quite possible he knew with whom she ran away.

"He spoke the truth," said Ulick. "I did not injure Janet in any way, nor did she leave home with me."

"I wonder who she went with?" said Irene. "Have you any idea?"

"How can I possibly know?" he said, evasively.

"No, of course not," she replied. "But I cannot understand why you will not come back to Hazelwell."

Warren Courtly joined them. He heard his wife's last remark, and remarked—

"You can have no reason for remaining away now you and the Squire are reconciled."

"I have an excellent reason," said Ulick, looking him straight in the face in a manner that made him feel very uncomfortable.

CHAPTER XIV

A DISCOVERY IMMINENT

Warren Courtly remained in London, and his wife returned home with the Squire. Irene was accustomed to his frequent absences from the Manor, and became somewhat reconciled to being alone. The Squire, however, was exceedingly angry with him, and ventured to remonstrate, but received no satisfaction from the interview; on the contrary, it tended to widen the breach between them.

Ulick promised his father he would return to Hazelwell as soon as circumstances permitted, and the Squire stated his intention of coming at the end of the month to see the Saint run in the Coronation Cup at Epsom.

Warren Courtly had a serious quarrel with Felix Hoffman over the letter he wrote to Irene. Felix, however, was master of the situation, and told him so.

"I know who you are, and that you have a wife at Anselm Manor; I wonder how she would take it if I introduced her to Mrs. Warren?"

"You dare not, you scoundrel," said Warren. "I have never lived with Mrs. Warren, you know it."

"I know she is no more Mrs. Warren than I am, unless you have committed bigamy, which is not at all likely," he replied.

"If you say one word to my wife about Mrs. Warren and myself, you will repent it," said Warren Courtly.

"Shall I? Then you will have to make it worth my while to hold my tongue," replied Felix.

"Turning blackmailer, are you?" said Warren. "What is your price?"

"Fifty pounds will carry me over this month, and I promise not to trouble you if I have good luck with it."

"And supposing you have bad luck?"

"Then I am afraid I must trespass upon your generosity again," replied Felix.

"And how long will this sort of thing go on?"

"It all depends upon circumstances. I may not require your assistance for some time."

"And if I refuse your request?"

"Then I shall feel it my duty to enlighten Mrs. Courtly."

There was no way out of the fix, so he paid Felix Hoffman fifty pounds, thankful to be able to keep him quiet for a time, until he could think over what was best to be done.

Why did he not make a clean breast of it to Irene? His folly was committed before he married her, and she could not blame him for attending to Janet's wants. It was shameful to leave Ulick under suspicion. Then he thought, "But he is not under suspicion now. I wonder why he does not go home. It is very curious. He cannot have discovered anything about me, that is almost impossible."

Ulick was half inclined to tax Warren with being the cause of all the trouble, and would have done so in all probability had a favourable opportunity occurred. Fortunately it did not, or angry words might have passed between them, which would have led to a serious quarrel.

Felix Hoffman had bad luck, and a few days after he received the fifty pounds he lost it all, and more with it. He had no hesitation in asking for assistance, which Warren point-blank refused.

"I see what you intend doing," he said, "and I do not mean to be bled. I will face the consequences, and you can do your worst."

Felix Hoffman was taken by surprise at the unexpectedly bold front shown, and said, angrily—

"Very well, you know what will happen."

"But you do not," replied Warren.

"I have a very good idea."

"I have told my wife everything, what do you think of that?"

"I don't believe it," said Felix, quaking lest it should be true.

"You may please yourself about that," Warren answered. "I have no desire to speak to you again."

"Then out of my house Mrs. Warren, or whoever she is, goes neck and crop."

Warren laughed provokingly, as he replied—

"It is not your house, and if anyone goes it will be yourself. I shall have great pleasure in assisting your mother to get rid of you, and I am sure it would be a relief to her."

Felix Hoffman went home in a towering rage. He owed a lot of money, and knew if he did not pay up that the bookmakers would show him scant courtesy. Some of them he had not treated well in his more prosperous days, and they would only be too glad to retaliate.

Mrs. Hoffman knew her son's temper was none of the best, and she saw he was in a bad humour. He did not, however, mean to let her into his secret as to the identity of Mr. Warren, nor had he any desire that Janet should leave the house; on the contrary, now he had calmed down, he was sorry he hinted at such a thing to Mr. Courtly.

He cudgelled his brains as to which was the best way to obtain money. He repaid the loan of five pounds to Mrs. Courtly in order to inspire her with confidence in him; he would write again and ask for a loan of five-and-twenty pounds; it was not much but it would be useful as a stop-gap.

He was careful over the composition of the letter, and anxiously awaited a reply. It came, and there was no money enclosed.

Mrs. Courtly wrote to the effect that her husband had warned her against him as an unprincipled cheat. She explained that she had shown his former letters to him, and that was his comment upon them. She had no desire to hold further communication with him.

This roused Felix Hoffman, and his anger for a time mastered him. He would make Warren Courtly pay dearly for this, and give his wife a shock she would not get over for a long time.

Janet little thought, as she sat reading a novel, what was going on in the next room.

Felix seized pen and paper, and commenced writing furiously. He read the letter when finished, and found it ridiculous. He must write in a calmer, more methodical and convincing strain, or she would take no notice of it.

At the end of an hour he had composed something that suited him. He could give her some information about her husband, and his goings on when in London, that would open her eyes, but he must be well paid for it, and have a hundred pounds down. He hinted that there was a lady in the case who went under the name of Mrs. Warren. "She resides with my mother, whose address I will send you if you forward me the amount I have named. I assure you what I write is true, and you can prove it for your own satisfaction. I have seen Mr. Courtly there many times with the lady named." There was more to the same purpose. "If that does not fetch her, I'll never write another letter," he said, with satisfaction at the thought that he was firing a mine that would explode in a manner Warren Courtly little dreamed of.

When Irene received the letter she was at first inclined to tear it up, but curiosity prevailed, and she read it. Her cheeks burned with anger. How dare this scoundrel make such a charge against Warren. Whatever he might do in the way of gambling and spending money foolishly, she was sure he would not deceive her as this man suggested.

She read the letter again, and became more uneasy. It was within her power to find out whether he had told her a lie or otherwise. Was it a ruse to get a hundred pounds out of her? That could hardly be the case, because the writer gave his address and was known to Warren, who could bring him to book for slandering him. She thought over his constant absence from home, his frequent visits to London, even when no racing was going on, his increased expenditure. Might not a portion of the money go in the manner suggested? Irene had very little knowledge of such matters, yet she had sense enough to perceive that if Warren was entangled much money would be required. She became restless and excited. Something must be done, she could not exist in this state of suspense. If Warren had deceived her, she would never live with him again.

Eventually she wrote, enclosing the amount required, and requesting Mrs. Hoffman's address.

Felix was delighted at the success of his scheme, and sent the same address he had given before.

"My mother lives with me," he wrote, "and Mrs. Warren is in the house. She is nearly always at home; but if you call and she happens to be out, my mother will attend to you. Ask to see Mrs. Warren."

"Living in the same house," thought Irene, "then it must be true. Oh, how miserable I am."

She made arrangements to go to London, taking her maid with her, and requesting Mrs. Dixon to inform Mr. Maynard of her departure. "Tell him I shall stay at the Walton with Warren, and that we shall probably remain until after Epsom week."

She had no idea whether Warren was at the Walton, or otherwise, because he always wrote from his club. She thought of the scented paper on which he had once written, and her heart sank.

Mary Marley, her maid, was surprised, but delighted at the prospect of a visit to London, for it was some time since she had been there.

Irene was silent during the journey, and went to bed early after dinner. Her maid was surprised her master was not there, but she made no remark. She knew her place. Next day Irene went out alone. She drove to Waterloo and booked to Feltham. Arriving at the station, she asked for Mrs. Hoffman at the address given. The porter directed her, and looked at her admiringly as she left the station, as it was seldom he saw such a stylishly dressed lady, and wondered who she could be.

Irene's heart beat painfully fast as she walked slowly along the road. The house was not far from the station the porter told her, and she dreaded reaching it. She felt half inclined to turn back. Perhaps it was some cunning trap laid for her by this man. She had read of the mysterious disappearances of women, and the prospect was not pleasant. She did not lack courage, and as she had come so far she would not turn back.

She reached the house, opened the gate, and rang the bell. Mrs. Hoffman opened the door.

"Does Mrs. Warren live here?" asked Irene, dreading her answer.

"Yes. She is out doing a little shopping at present. Will you come in, my lady?" said Mrs. Hoffman, overwhelmed at the sight of such expensive raiment and at Irene's aristocratic features.

"Thank you, I am anxious to see her," she said, as she entered the house, feeling that her life was about to be shattered, and all her fears realised, before she left it again.

Mrs. Hoffman opened the door of the front room, and said—

"This is Mrs. Warren's sitting-room; I am sure she will not be long."

Irene thanked her and sat down. As she did not seem inclined to talk, Mrs. Hoffman discreetly withdrew, although she would dearly have loved to linger and gossip.

Irene looked round the room curiously. It was neatly furnished, but there was nothing to give her a clue as to the identity of its occupier, nor did she see anything indicative of Warren's frequent presence in the house. She was relieved at this; after all, there might be some mistake, and she could apologise and leave. She would willingly have given another hundred pounds to find out she had been deceived by Felix Hoffman, and allowed him to go scot free into the bargain.

Irene moved about the room looking at sundry books and papers lying about on the table. She saw no signs of work-basket, or anything to indicate that Mrs. Warren was industrious, and again her hopes sank.

Time passed slowly, and she commenced to feel uneasy. She was inclined to leave the house. She rang the bell and Mrs. Hoffman appeared.

"Do you think Mrs. Warren will be much longer?" she asked. "Perhaps I had better call again, but as I came from London I am anxious to see her."

"I expected her in before this," said Mrs. Hoffman. "Perhaps you had better wait as you have come so far."

"Will Mr. Warren be with her?"

"Oh, dear no; he seldom comes now," said Mrs. Hoffman.

Irene was thankful for this; it was a grain of comfort, and she anxiously caught at any straw.

"They do not live together," said the gossiping woman, "but the separation is by mutual consent. They quarrel occasionally when he is here, and he always seems glad to get away. Mrs. Warren is a nice lady, I like her very much, but of course you know her?"

"Of course," echoed Irene.

"And her husband?"

"Yes."

"I wonder who she is?" thought Mrs. Hoffman. "She's not in the same circle as Mrs. Warren, that's certain. How did she find out the address?"

"Mrs. Warren sent you her address I suppose?" asked Mrs. Hoffman.

"I knew it," was Irene's answer, "or I should not have been here."

Mrs. Hoffman felt it would be indiscreet to put further questions on this matter. She heard the gate click and said—

"I expect this is Mrs. Warren. I will mention you are here. What name, please, my lady?"

"Do not tell her anyone has called to see her," replied Irene, hastily, "it will be a pleasant surprise for her, as she does not expect me."

CHAPTER XV

THE RESULT OF THE DISCOVERY

"You have been a long time," said Mrs. Hoffman to Janet.

"I went for a walk through the Park; it is such a nice morning," she replied.

Irene heard her voice and started at the sound. It was familiar. Where had she heard it before? She felt she was on the verge of a startling discovery, and became agitated. She determined not to appear at a disadvantage, and therefore controlled her feelings.

Janet entered, unaware there was anyone in the room, and as Irene was hidden from view behind the opened door she did not see her. She walked to the table to put down a parcel and Irene saw her. At first she was too bewildered to speak; then she said sharply—

"Janet, what are you doing here?"

Janet Todd looked round, frightened and startled at the unexpected question. When she saw Irene she staggered back and sank into a chair, covered with shame and confusion. She made no answer, and Irene stood looking at her, still unable to grasp the full meaning of the situation.

"How is it you are living here?" she asked. "Are you a friend of Mrs. Hoffman or Mrs. Warren?"

Janet looked at her with tears in her eyes, and said, in a broken voice—

"Oh, why have you come here? Please go away and leave me; I am a miserable, wretched woman."

It was far from Irene's intention to leave her without learning the truth. The appearance of Janet was totally unexpected, and she could not account for it.

"I shall not leave you until you tell me why you are in this house, and who induced you to leave your home. I know it was not Mr. Maynard."

"It was not; he is a good, brave man, and would never wrong any woman," said Janet. "I cannot tell you why I am here—I dare not."

"I was told to ask for Mrs. Warren. Where is she?"

"Who told you to ask for her?"

"That does not matter." Then it suddenly occurred to her that Janet might be Mrs. Warren, and the thought seemed to freeze the blood in her veins. She came forward and, bending over her, said in a low voice—

"You are not Mrs. Warren, are you? Tell me you are not, Janet, for pity's sake."

She made no reply, but sobbed convulsively, her body shook, and she shivered painfully.

"Are you Mrs. Warren?" asked Irene again, in a tone which demanded an answer.

"Yes," faintly sobbed Janet.

"And Mr. Warren is my husband. Janet, how could you do me such a bitter wrong? I have always been your friend," said Irene.

Despite the trouble and confusion she was in, Janet saw there was a misunderstanding, and she must do all in her power to make the best of things.

"I did not wrong you," said Janet. "I ran away with Mr. Courtly before you were married to him. If there be any wrong, you did it to me by taking the place I ought to have occupied."

Irene started; Janet was putting a different complexion on the case.

"So it was my husband who induced you to leave your home?" she asked.

"Yes, and he promised to marry me."

"And you believed him?"

"Yes."

"Did you leave your father's house with him the night Mr. Maynard had the quarrel about you?"

"I did."

"You saw him that night?"

"Yes, and he told me everything, but forbid me to speak about it to the Squire. He was very angry, and said his father had no right to accuse him, and that he would not return to Hazelwell until he asked his forgiveness."

"Did you tell him you had arranged to leave home with Mr. Courtly?"

"No, I dare not; he would have told my father, and I should have been detained."

"And you have known all this time that suspicion rested upon Mr. Maynard, and that he was suspected of having gone away with you?" asked Irene.

"That is so, but he has forbidden me to speak about it."

"He knows you are here!" exclaimed Irene.

"Promise you will not mention it to anyone, and I will tell you all," said Janet.

Irene sat down and, as she did so, said—

"If I promise I will not mention what you tell me to anyone but my husband, will that satisfy you?"

"Why inform him?"

"Because I may find it necessary," said Irene.

"It will be better not to do so."

"I am the best judge of that," she replied.

Janet then gave Irene a full account of her life since leaving home with Warren Courtly, and how Ulick had called to see her, after accidentally catching sight of her in Feltham, and of his presence in the house when Warren Courtly called.

"Mr. Maynard knows all?" exclaimed Irene, in consternation.

"Everything," replied Janet, "and he was most anxious you should not discover the truth. He will be very angry if he finds out I have told you."

Then it was to save her pain and shame Ulick had allowed the blame to rest upon his shoulders, knowing at the same time her husband was guilty. Why had he done this for her sake? Her heart answered her, and she knew he loved her and that she loved him. What a mistake it had all been. The Squire had blundered, and Ulick had thrown away his chance of happiness and her own by his hasty conduct. It was done, and could not be undone, and she must bear it as well as she was able. How she wished Janet had told him, the night he left Hazelwell, that she was about to leave her home with Warren Courtly. Ulick would have prevented it, and everything would have been so different.

It was some time before she spoke; then she asked—

"What is my husband to you now?"

"Nothing," said Janet, colouring. "Since he married you we have lived entirely apart. You can believe what I say. I have no love for him, he has none for me. He makes me an allowance, which he has a right to do. We are not even good friends, and I do not care if I never see him again. I was a vain, foolish girl when I ran away with him, and have bitterly repented it ever since. Mr. Maynard told me my father was anxious for me to return home, and he strongly advised me to do so, until he discovered who Mr. Warren was; then for your sake he bade me keep silent and remain where I am."

Irene was somewhat relieved at this. From Janet's statement she gathered her husband had been faithful to her since their marriage, and that, to a great extent, condoned his offence towards herself, but she could not forgive him for so cowardly allowing the blame to rest upon Ulick. The contrast between the two came vividly before her. Her husband hiding his wrongs by sacrificing a friend; Ulick Maynard knowingly bearing the blame to shield her from sorrow and shame. She felt sorely tempted to go to Ulick, fling herself into his arms, and ask him to take her away from it all. She knew he would resist this temptation for her sake, and after a moment's consideration she also knew it was impossible for her to act in such a manner.

"We must keep this interview to ourselves," said Irene. "No one must know of my visit, and you must tell Mrs. Hoffman I am a friend, any name will suffice to satisfy her. I am very sorry for you, Janet, and advise you to return to your father."

"I cannot. Mr. Maynard made me promise not to do so until he gave me permission, and I could not face the people in Helton after what has happened."

"You will live that down," said Irene. "I will take care no one talks about you, as far as I am able, and I can do a good deal to help you."

"It is very kind of you," replied Janet, "and I hope some day to see my father and live with him again. I am not so bad, and I have kept myself respectable since I ran away."

"I quite believe that," replied Irene. "Do you think my husband will call here again?"

"I hardly know; he has posted me money lately. I have no desire to see him," replied Janet.

"You will oblige me by not seeing him," said Irene. "Forbid him the house. If you require money write to me, and I will send it."

"He might see the letter and recognise my handwriting."

"That is of no consequence. If he does he will soon learn I have seen you and know everything," said Irene.

"I will write and tell him I wish him to keep away from the house, and I feel sure he will do as I desire," said Janet.

Irene remained some time longer, for they had much to talk about. When she was leaving Janet said she would write to her at once if there was anything of importance she thought she ought to know.

When Irene returned to the Walton, her maid told her Warren Courtly had called, and was very angry when he discovered his wife had come up to London without informing him.

114

"The manager told him you were here," said Mary. "I expect he thought he had come to see you."

"Did you see Mr. Courtly?"

"Yes, and he asked me where you had gone. I told him I did not know, but that I expected you back in the afternoon, and he said he would be here for dinner."

Irene went to her room, and after dismissing her maid thought over the best course to pursue. Should she tell him of her meeting with Janet, and that she had learned everything, or would it be better to leave him in the dark? What excuse could she give for her journey to London? State she had come to give him a pleasant surprise, and that the Squire would be there in a day or two for the Epsom week. Perhaps that would be the better plan. If he was unreasonably cross and irritable, she might possibly throw out a hint that would startle him and make him more careful.

It was four o'clock, and she did not expect him for dinner before seven, so there was ample time to review the eventful morning she had spent with Janet Todd. This she was doing when her maid knocked at the door and said Mr. Ulick Maynard had called to see her.

Irene did not expect him, his father must have written at once to inform him she had gone to town.

"Where is he?" asked Irene.

"In the reading-room."

"I will see him in my sitting-room," she said; and her maid went away to give the necessary instruction.

"I am glad to see you," said Ulick, as she entered the room. "It is an unexpected pleasure. I had no idea you were in town until my father wrote me a hurried note."

She shook hands with him, and as she did so the thought that he knew what her husband had done, and how he had acted, caused her some confusion, at which Ulick wondered.

"I came to town to give Warren a surprise," she said, hurriedly. "I have not seen him yet, but he has called, and my maid says he did not seem overwhelmed with joy at my presence."

"Then he ought to have been," said Ulick.

"He is joining me at dinner. Will you make one of the party?" she asked.

"If you wish it, and you think he will have no objection?"

"I am sure he will be pleased to see you."

"In that case I have no hesitation in accepting. I will run home and dress."

How lovely Irene looked; he felt he must go away, leave her presence, or he would be tempted to betray his feelings. He little knew how strongly she controlled herself, and how deeply she loved him. It was well for them that it should be so.

Warren Courtly's temper had not improved when he arrived again at the Walton. He went to Irene's room and waited impatiently for her, and she did not keep him long.

"What brings you to town in such a hurry?" he asked.

"I felt lonely and thought I would give you a surprise," she said, with a faint smile.

"You had no business to come without first writing me about it."

"I saw no harm in it."

"Harm, no; but it is a strange proceeding on your part," he replied.

"Are you not pleased to see me?" she asked.

"Of course I am," he answered, testily. "It's the manner of your coming I do not approve of."

"You will soon recover from the shock," she said, carelessly. "Shall we dine at seven. I have invited Ulick Maynard to join us. He called this afternoon, and I thought it only polite. He accepted on condition you had no objection, and I said you would be very pleased to see him."

Warren Courtly with difficulty suppressed an oath. Of late he had avoided Ulick, and he was the last man he cared to meet.

116

"I would rather have had you to myself," he said.

"Ulick is such an old friend, he will make no difference," she replied.

"You are precious fond of his society still," he said, showing his ill-temper; "I should have thought you would have preferred being alone with me, if you came down to give me a surprise. Perhaps you wrote and informed him you were coming here."

Irene was angry at this remark, and said—

"You know I did no such thing, and I am surprised at you insulting me by such a remark. His father wrote and gave him the information."

"At your suggestion," sneered Warren.

"You are in a bad temper, and forget yourself," she replied. "I will leave you to recover your manners. Remember one thing, if you make any more suggestions of a similar kind at dinner I shall retaliate. I am quite capable of giving you a very unpleasant surprise if you fail to treat me with respect."

She went out of the room, and he stood looking at the closed door. Then he said to himself—

"What has come over her? I never found her in this mood before. I must get to the bottom of it. Retaliate, will she? Well, we shall see."

CHAPTER XVI

A RACE TO BE REMEMBERED

It was not a social meal, anything but that, and they were glad when it was over. Warren Courtly, irritable and ill at ease, spoke once or twice to his wife in such a manner that Ulick glared at him savagely; he noticed it, and enjoyed it.

Unfortunately, Warren was going from bad to worse. He realised the truth of the saying that evil communications corrupt good manners. At his club he played bridge and lost large sums. On the racecourse he tried to repair these losses, with the inevitable result. His fortune, at one time ample, gradually dwindled away, and he knew that if he did not pull up Anselm Manor would be in the market in a couple of years or so.

Irene had no idea things were as bad as this; her mind was occupied with other matters. The knowledge she possessed of her husband's conduct towards Janet Todd and Ulick she found burdensome. She was positively certain Ulick would not tell the Squire, and she felt he ought to know, but she had promised Janet to tell no one but her husband. When she left them to retire for the night, Warren commenced to talk about racing. He had a substantial bet about Sandstone for the Derby at very fair odds, and was sanguine of winning. He discussed the race with Ulick, who was of the same opinion that Sandstone would win.

"If he does," Ulick remarked, "I should put part of the winnings on my horse for the Coronation Cup."

"Your horse!" exclaimed Warren. "I had no idea you owned one."

"More than one—several," replied Ulick; "but the Saint is the best."

"You own the Saint!" said Warren, more and more surprised. "I have heard it said he is the best three-year-old we have."

"He is not far short of it," he replied. "At least, that is the opinion of Fred May, and he is a very good judge."

"You are lucky to own such a colt. Where did you pick him up?"

Ulick explained how he came to possess him, and Warren said, grumbling, that some people had all the luck.

"I have been deuced unfortunate of late," he went on, "and a big win is the only way out of the difficulty that I can see. If Sandstone lands the Derby I will have a plunge on your horse. I am much obliged to you for telling me."

"I shall be glad to hear of your winning a good round sum," replied Ulick. "I was sorry to hear you were compelled to part with Holme Farm."

Warren's face clouded. He had heard quite enough about that, and said—

"I don't see what there is to make such a fuss about. Something had to go; why not that part of the estate as well as another?"

"My father says he would have given you half as much again for it."

"I could not have accepted it; he would merely have done it out of kindness."

Ulick thought this probable, and knew his father would do that, and more, for Irene's sake.

The Squire arrived at the Walton, and was feverishly anxious for the Saint's race to be decided. Fred May had sent glowing accounts of the colt's progress, and considered he had a chance second to none.

"We will show them what he is capable of this time; it will be the race of his life. He has never been quite so fit as he is now, and I fear nothing, not even Vulture," he wrote.

"By Jove! that is good news," said the Squire. "The olive green will win, my boy."

119

On Derby Day they all went to Epsom, where Redmond Maynard had a box, and the great scene was repeated as it has been for many years.

It was one of the sights of the world, most uncomfortable, but unique.

Sandstone won somewhat easily, and Warren was jubilant. He meant to invest the bulk of his winnings on the Saint.

He confided to Irene that if Ulick's colt won his difficulties would be well-nigh at an end.

"I had no idea you were in difficulties," she said.

"Not very serious," he replied, in an off-hand manner, which did not deceive her, "but still bad enough to be unpleasant."

Thursday, the day after the Derby, was fixed for the Coronation Cup, and the half-dozen horses that were likely to go to the post were all great performers.

It was a meeting of champions, a race to be remembered, and a thorough sporting affair. The crowd was much larger than usual on this day, and the race was looked forward to with as much eagerness as the Derby had been the previous day.

Warren Courtly was in a fever of excitement. He had backed the Saint to win him several thousands, and when he saw him in the paddock felt inclined to put more on.

The colt's peculiar colour rendered him easily distinguishable, and he was mobbed in the paddock, taking it as unconcernedly as usual.

Ben Sprig was to ride him again, and he felt a trifle anxious as to the result. He had never been beaten on the Saint, having scored five victories in succession; but he knew the five horses he was to meet in about a quarter of an hour were probably the best in the country.

Vulture had won the Derby the previous year, as easily as Sandstone, and followed it up by a St. Leger victory. Coralie, a handsome mare, had an Ascot Gold Cup to her credit. Avenger made hacks of the last Cesarewitch field. Decoy Duck was an Eclipse winner; and Mermaid landed the Oaks in Vulture's year. Well might

120

men gasp and exclaim, "What a field. It beats the Derby into a cocked hat."

No wonder the betting was fast and furious, and backers were split up into half-a-dozen parties. It was the more venturesome speculators who stood by the Saint. The old hands preferred one of the other tried stayers.

"It is too much to expect of him," they said of the Saint. "It's more than Sandstone could do, and look how he won the Derby yesterday."

Vulture was favourite, then Coralie and Avenger, and the Saint figured at eight to one.

"It is a real good price," said the Squire. "I must have a hundred on," and when he had booked that he longed for more, hesitated a moment or two, and then doubled it.

Irene caught the fever and made Warren put a "pony" on for her.

Ulick had a small amount going, and Warren had plunged.

Cautious Fred May departed from his usual custom of having "a tenner on" and invested fifty, and had done the same for Ben Sprig, who was not supposed to indulge in such iniquitous practices, for fear of the far-reaching arm of the stewards of the Jockey Club. Ben was a cautious man, and could conscientiously say he had never made a wager in his life—it was always done for him.

Great was the excitement as the horses went on to the course. Vulture, wearing the stars and stripes of his American owner, was first out, his jockey sitting crouched on his withers—an ugly sight, but often effective. Then came the handsome Coralie, in purple and scarlet, followed by Avenger's yellow and red cap, with Decoy Duck and Mermaid close behind.

"There's only five of 'em," said one spectator. "Where's the other? What is it?"

"The Saint, of course; Ben Sprig's up, he's always last out."

The Saint cantered slowly down as the others galloped past, and Ben, whipping him round, followed in the rear before half the onlookers were aware the colt had come out of the paddock.

Away they went to the famous Derby starting-post. Here Vulture showed his scant respect for decorum by lashing out all round, and in a final flourish tried to dash through the tapes, but did not succeed.

After a quarter of an hour wasted by these vagaries on the part of the favourite, the half-dozen started on their journey.

Coralie dashed off with the lead, followed by Vulture and Avenger, with the other three close up. It was evident it was to be a race from start to finish between the lot. They disappeared from view, and as they came in sight again, the mare still led, and the horses ran wide. The half-dozen were all on terms with each other. Tattenham Corner was reached and the crowd on the new stand cheered wildly as they swept past. It was here that Ben Sprig always looked out for a chance of gaining a few lengths. He wanted them more than ever on this occasion, and meant getting them if possible. He hugged the rails, and kept the Saint well in hand. He lost no ground but he gained none, as they were all adopting similar tactics, and none of the horses ran wide. The half-dozen seemed dangerously heaped together as they rounded the bend, and the crowd on that part of the course anticipated a spill, but happily it did not occur. Coralie led down the hill, the purple and gold glittering and shining royally in the sunlight.

The party in the Squire's box were unusually excited, which was not to be wondered at. Fred May was invited to join them, and he was more anxious than he had ever been before over the result of a race.

He had said he "feared nothing," with the Saint, and meant it. If he had a dread of one, it was Vulture, for he knew him to be a great horse, despite his temper.

"They keep their places," said the Squire, "but I fancy the Saint is drawing up a trifle."

Warren Courtly was very pale, and his hand shook as he held his glasses. Irene glanced at him, and thought—

"Much depends on this race, or he would not be like that." She turned to Ulick, who stood at her side, and said, "You take it coolly, are you confident of winning?"

"Yes, I think he will win; I know Ben is riding a splendid race, and saving him for the finish up the rise. That is where it tells."

"I do hope he will win, Ulick," she said.

He looked into her eyes and read more than he dared hope for.

Coralie had run well, but now they were racing in deadly earnest.

Vulture wrested the lead from her, and his giant stride told its tale. He shot out like a greyhound, and a great shout greeted the favourite's move. Avenger was close on his heels, and Ben was gradually creeping up with the Saint.

They were in the hollow now, in full view of the crowded stands, and the battle was watched with the greatest interest.

Not more than five lengths between the six horses—a sight seldom seen in such a race. Decoy Duck and Mermaid were in the rear.

"I am afraid he will hardly do it," said the Squire, "but what a race it is; there will be no disgrace in being beaten."

Warren Courtly bit his lip and looked desperate. Would the Saint get up and win? It seemed impossible; and yet the trainer and Ulick looked confident, so there must be a chance. The victory of Ulick's horse meant much to him, of his defeat he dare not think.

Seething with excitement, the vast crowd surged wildly, and roar after roar proclaimed the desperate nature of the struggle.

Ben Sprig knew the time had come when he must ask the Saint to go one better than he had ever done before. He knew what a good colt he was, he never doubted his courage, but in front of him was Vulture, a more than ordinary Derby winner, Avenger, the Newmarket crack, and the handsome Coralie. He knew he had the Ascot Cup winner at his mercy, he fancied Avenger would have to play second fiddle to the Saint, but what about Vulture? Would he be able to catch him, and, if he did, beat him? For the first time since he had ridden the Saint he doubted. Vulture was three lengths ahead, and striding along without a falter. It seemed almost impossible to catch him, but Ben knew the impossible often became the possible with a good horse. Win he must; the Saint should not lower his colours; the olive green should never strike to the stars and stripes, and he, Ben Sprig, the exponent of the old school of riding, would not succumb to the efforts of that crouching little Yankee in front of him. Ben felt the blood tingle in his veins, and his heart beat fast.

The Saint felt his grip, and knew it meant mischief. The colt was full of fire, he never had flinched, and he never would.

Who that saw it will ever forget that memorable moment on a memorable day? Who that heard them will forget the ringing cheers, the shouts of victory? Who forget the sight of that flash of olive green, which seemed to shoot forward with lightning speed? Ben Sprig fancied he was being hurled through space; even he had never expected this of the Saint.

Ulick's colt passed Coralie like a flash, drew level with Avenger, beat him, and ran up to the Vulture's quarters before people had time to grasp the wonderful feat.

Fred May shouted for joy; he forgot he was a trainer, and therefore expected to regard everything as a matter of course. Ulick shouted, the Squire waved his hat, Warren Courtly sat down, the strain was too great, and Irene felt a peculiar swimming sensation in her head.

Vulture's jockey was not caught napping—Americans seldom are—and he rode his best, but he had met his match. The grim determination of the elder man was not to be denied. Ben Sprig felt his honour was at stake, he must "beat this kid." The two magnificent thoroughbreds struggled desperately, they fought for victory as only "blue bloods" can, and they knew what it all meant as well as the riders. There is no sight in the world so thrilling as the final struggle of two gallant racehorses; it is the highest form of sport, the most soul-stirring scene a man can behold; he becomes part and parcel of the battle going on before his eyes.

Vulture and the Saint were level, the stars and stripes and the olive green were locked together. Only for a second or two it lasted, and then Ulick's colt gained the vantage, and "Mr. Lanark's" champion won the Coronation Cup by a short head, after one of the grandest struggles ever witnessed on any course.

CHAPTER XVII

THE SQUIRE OVERHEARS

The Saint's wonderful victory was the chief topic of conversation for the remainder of the afternoon, and it was discussed all over the course. It was acknowledged to have surpassed the Derby victory of Sandstone, and the merits of the pair were a fruitful source of conversation. Perhaps Warren Courtly had as much reason to rejoice as anyone over the Saint's win, for he had landed a large stake. He left the box and went into the ring, where he met several acquaintances, who congratulated him.

Felix Hoffman stood alone in the paddock, his face gloomy and desperate. He had been hard hit again, his bad luck stuck to him, and he had lost the hundred pounds he received from Irene. He had plunged on Vulture and lost, and cursed "the curiosity" for beating him.

The Squire and his companions went down to the paddock to see the winner, and congratulate Ben Sprig.

Warren was not with them, but he followed later on.

Ulick and Irene returned to the box, as she was anxious to sit down and rest after the excitement of the race.

The Squire stood talking with the trainer and Ben Sprig, and Warren Courtly was coming towards them when he encountered Felix Hoffman.

He tried to avoid him, but Felix was in a desperate plight, and meant to obtain assistance somehow.

"Had any luck?" he asked.

"Yes," replied Warren.

"I'm dead broke; lend me a tenner to try and get a bit back."

"Not a farthing," replied Warren, who moved on, but stopped when he found Felix Hoffman following him, and said, angrily—

"Go away, I will have nothing to do with you."

"You must help me; I have done a lot of dirty work for you."

Warren was losing his temper, and his eyes had an angry gleam in them.

"If you pester me I shall give you in charge; go away."

Still Felix held his ground, and said—

"I only ask for a trifle; it will pay you to give it me."

"Get out of my way or I will knock you down," was the reply.

The Squire, walking across the paddock talking to Ben Sprig, was so engrossed he failed to notice them.

"Knock me down, will you?" said Felix. "I'd like to see you do it. If you don't do as I ask, I'll go straight to your wife and tell her all about your dealings with Mrs. Warren. She's here; I saw her in the box with you."

Warren raised his hand and in another moment would have struck him, but the Squire heard the words, and held his arm back in time to prevent the blow.

"Who is this fellow?" asked the Squire.

"Felix Hoffman is my name, at your service."

"Do you know him?" he said to Warren.

"Oh, yes; he knows me very well," answered Felix.

"I did not address you," replied the Squire; and repeated his question.

Warren nodded as he said, "Unfortunately I do; he is a regular scoundrel."

"I am not as bad as you," was Felix's retort. "I haven't got one wife; you have two."

"What does the man mean?" asked the Squire.

"He's a fool, or worse; come away from him," said Warren, "or I shall do him an injury."

"I don't know who you are," said Felix, addressing the Squire; "but if you are his father-in-law I can tell you he is a bad lot. His wife, Mrs. Warren, lives with my mother, and that is the address; you can call and see for yourself," he said, as he handed him a card.

Warren snatched it out of his hand and tore it up.

"Give me another card," said the Squire, and Felix handed one to him, Warren not daring to interfere on this occasion.

They moved away from Felix Hoffman, and the Squire said—

"What is the meaning of this? Is there any truth in it?"

"He's a confounded liar," said Warren, angrily.

Felix Hoffman heard him, and said—

"I am not. If you want to learn the truth, ask his wife; she knows all about it."

Warren stepped up to him in fury, struck him a heavy blow on the mouth, and knocked him down.

Fortunately a race was being run at the time, and there were only a few people in the paddock. The Squire forced Warren away with him, and they left Felix sprawling on the grass.

"You ought not to have struck him," said the Squire.

"He deserved it."

"Was there any truth in what he said?"

"No, none whatever. It is true I have been to his house, and that a Mrs. Warren lives there, but I have nothing to do with her, you may rest assured of that."

"He said Irene knew all about it."

"Which is absurd, because there is nothing to know. That is

127

the man who wrote the begging-letter Irene showed you, and you said the matter ought to be placed in the hands of the police."

"The scoundrel; he deserves all he got and more," said the Squire.

Warren was relieved at this change of front, and said—

"He once gave me a winner at Hurst Park, and he has pestered me for money ever since. He was asking me to lend him ten pounds just before you came up. It was because I refused he trumped up this story about Mrs. Warren. It is all a fabrication."

"I am glad to hear it," answered the Squire, not quite satisfied.

Warren went into the ring, and when the Squire entered the box Ulick left Irene in his charge.

"We have had rather an unpleasant scene in the paddock," said the Squire; "that fellow Hoffman, who wrote to you, insulted Warren, and he knocked him down. It served him right."

Irene turned pale and said, in an agitated voice—

"What did he say?"

"Told a pack of lies about Warren and some woman living at his house. I don't believe a word of it," said the Squire. "He gave me his address and told me to go and find out for myself. Here it is," and he handed her the card.

Irene was in desperate straits. He must be prevented from visiting Mrs. Hoffman's house at any cost.

"Of course, you will take no notice of it," she said.

"The fellow actually said you knew all about it, but I did not believe him. By gad, if I thought Warren had deceived you I would make things hot for him."

"He has not deceived me," she replied. "Please do me a favour; take no further notice of the matter."

"Warren snatched the first card he offered me out of his hand. Why did he do that?" asked the Squire.

"No doubt he thought it an insult for him to offer it to you," she replied.

"That may have been the reason. I hope so," he replied.

A feeling of depression seemed to have come over them, and Ulick, who had returned, said—

"I am afraid the excitement has been too much for you all. Shall we go home, there are only two more races?"

They readily agreed, with the exception of Warren, who said he would see it out and return after the last race.

This irritated the Squire, but he made no remark, and they left him to his own devices.

Warren immediately sent a telegram to Janet telling her to go away at once, as the Squire had her address.

Janet was surprised at this, but she wondered still more when another wire came from Irene to the same effect, and asking her to send an address to the Walton.

The Squire, however, had no intention of going to Feltham, and when he returned to Hazelwell Janet went back to Mrs. Hoffman's.

Warren Courtly felt he had better make a clean breast of it. He would tell Irene all, and trust to her generosity to forgive him.

A week after the races, when they had returned to Anselm Manor, Warren Courtly said to his wife—

"Irene, I have something to tell you: it is humiliating for me to have to confess that I have done wrong, and it will cause you pain to hear my story."

She knew what he was about to say, but thought it better to allow him to tell his own story. She was glad he made her his confidante, and confessed his fault. She felt she could almost forgive him. To love him was impossible, for her heart was not in her own keeping.

"You recollect when Janet Todd disappeared from home?"

"And Ulick Maynard was, and still is by many people, suspected of wronging her," she said.

"He did not wrong her, he is perfectly innocent. It was before I became on intimate terms with you that I was infatuated with Janet. She was pretty and attracted me, and gradually we drifted together, until we became more than mere friends. I persuaded her to leave home and go to London. She is there now, and I have never deserted her, or let her want for anything. When I knew you, Irene, and loved you, I severed all connection with Janet, and we have been almost strangers to each other ever since our marriage. Can you forgive me for what I have done? It would have been unpardonable had I continued to see Janet, but I have only done so when she requested more money than I thought necessary."

He felt relieved now he had told her, and waited for her reply.

"I have not much to forgive," she said. "It is Ulick Maynard who has been wronged. You must tell the Squire all."

"Never," he exclaimed.

"Then I shall be compelled to do so, to clear Ulick. That reparation you owe him, if not more," she said, firmly.

"I would not have told you had I thought you would act like this."

"It was needless; I knew all. I have seen Janet, and she has confessed everything to me," was Irene's reply.

He looked amazed. "You have seen her!" he exclaimed. "How did you find her out?"

"Felix Hoffman sent me her address, for a consideration."

"So you have been spying on me, playing the lady detective. I am much obliged to you, and am sorry I confessed my fault," he said, sneeringly.

"When you confessed I admired you for it; you are changing my opinion of you," she replied.

"I forbid you to tell the Squire. Perhaps you would like to confide in Ulick, you appear to be very good friends?"

130

"It would be useless, he already knows everything," she said, quietly.

Warren Courtly felt decidedly small, but he hardly believed her.

"He knows nothing," he said.

"He does, for he was in her house on one occasion when you called to see Janet. He heard her story, and for my sake forbade her to speak of it, or return home," she said.

"For your sake," he said, sarcastically. "Did he tell you this?"

"No; Ulick is far too honourable for that," she replied, hotly. "He is not mean or underhand. Janet gave me the information."

"Which, no doubt, you were glad to receive," he said.

"I was, for it proved there was at least one man in the world who thought me worthy of sacrifices on his part," she answered, bitterly.

"If he knows I took Janet away, why does he not tell his father?" asked Warren.

"He will never tell him."

"Because he loves you?" said Warren.

"And if he does?" she asked, proudly. "What then? Am I not worthy to be loved by a good man?"

"Do you return his love?" he asked, savagely.

"Yes," she said, calmly.

He laughed harshly, as he replied—

"Then you have no cause to complain of my conduct with Janet."

"You degrade yourself and me by speaking in that manner. You know that Ulick has no knowledge that I love him, or is aware that I know he loves me. I am your wife and will do my duty. You will have no cause to complain, all the wrong is on your side," she said.

"Tell the Squire if you like," he said. "Only remember, if you do I shall sell Anselm Manor and leave the country, and you will go with me. You are my wife, and must obey me."

"That is a threat you will never carry out," she said.

"I will; so you can think it over. There is another thing I wish to mention. If you inform the Squire, I will make matters very unpleasant for yourself and Ulick. I have ample grounds for suspicion."

She did not deign to answer him, but walked proudly out of the room.

"So he knows," thought Warren, moodily. "What a coward he must think me. I'll prove to him I am not one before this year is out, how or when I do not know, but I'll do it."

He went into the stable yard and mounted a horse that stood ready saddled.

Irene saw him ride away at a breakneck pace, and wondered where he was going. After all, he was her husband, and she felt anxious about him. She knew how he would feel about Ulick, and dreaded the consequences. She wished she had spoken more kindly to him, but he insulted her with his implied suspicions.

As the evening wore on, and he did not return, she became more and more uneasy.

It was after eleven when she heard the sound of horse's hoofs coming up the drive, and shortly after Warren entered the room.

"I am glad you have returned," she said, softly. "I was anxious about you. I spoke harshly to you, perhaps, but I was excited, and hardly knew what I said. If you wish I will not tell the Squire about Janet."

He was surprised at her words. His ride had done him good, the gallop across country had aroused him to a better frame of mind.

"I thought you would not care what became of me," he said. "When I can screw up my courage I will tell the Squire Ulick is innocent, but I cannot do it yet. Give me a little time, Irene, and all will come right in the end."

"I hope so," she said. "Do not be reckless because we have quarrelled. Let us make the best of things as they are. I am very glad to hear you have decided to tell the Squire all, it is the very best thing you can do, and I am sure it will be a relief to you."

CHAPTER XVIII

"TALLY-HO!"

The year passed rapidly away, and the hunting season was in full swing. The Rushshire hounds were to meet at Hazelwell, and Ulick saw the fixture in the paper.

"By Jove! I should like to have a spin with them again," he said to himself; "it is more than two years since I had a rousing gallop over our country. I cannot go to Hazelwell, but I have a good mind to join them as they pass through Helton village on the way to Brecon Wood. I'll write to Eli and ask him to put me up for the night, and he will be able to give me a mount. My father will be out with the hounds, and many people will recognise me, but I can vanish when the hunt is over. It will be amusing to see how the good folks take it, and whether they object to my presence."

He wrote to Eli, who was in a flutter of excitement when he received the letter. Of course, he would give him a bed, and be glad to see him. "If I could only get Random for him to ride," he said to himself, "that would be a treat. I'll try it on, anyway."

He rode over to Anselm Manor and fortunately found Irene alone. To her he showed Ulick's letter and she was delighted to hear he was coming down.

"I have come to ask a favour of you," said Eli.

"I shall have much pleasure in granting it, if I can," she replied, with a smile.

"Will you lend me Random to mount him on?" he asked.

"I shall be delighted," she replied. Then she wondered what Warren would say, as he would be sure to inquire where the horse was. She could tell him she had lent him to Eli for a friend to ride, as she did not intend to hunt that day, but merely to be at the breakfast at Hazelwell.

"You can take him back with you now; one of the grooms can ride over," she said.

Eli was delighted at the success of his plan, and as he looked at Random in his box, said—

"You will be surprised to have your old master on your back, but I expect you will know him again."

Ulick arrived at the Hazelwell stud farm, and Eli greeted him heartily.

"Something tells me you will not leave us again," he said.

"You are wrong, Eli; I cannot go to Hazelwell yet, not until—— " he hesitated.

"Not until what?" asked Eli.

"Until the man who ran away with Janet thinks fit to confess to my father," said Ulick.

"Then you will have to wait a long time," said Eli, "for he has not got it in him."

"You know him!" exclaimed Ulick.

"Not for certain, but I have a very good idea. We will not talk about that. Have you heard anything of Janet?"

"Yes," said Ulick. "She is well, and I know is leading a respectable life, but she cannot come home at present, and does not wish you to see her until she has asked you to forgive her."

"I am glad to hear that, it is good news; but I should like to have her here again. If you know where she is, tell her I have forgiven her long ago." He did not ask why she did not come home, but her refusal to do so confirmed his suspicions, and he thought he understood her reason for remaining away, and approved of it.

"I have a good mount for you," said Eli. "Would you like to see him, or will you wait until the morning?"

"We may as well look at him now," said Ulick, "and then I can dream of one of the best runs on record."

135

They went out and across the yard, Eli lighting the way with a lantern. He opened the door of a box near to that in which Ulick entered the night he gave him such a surprise.

Holding up the light, Eli said—

"He's not a bad sort, is he?"

At first Ulick did not recognise the horse, as the light was not particularly good. He stepped up to his side, and Random sniffed and pushed his head against him.

"He seems to know me," said Ulick. Then, as he took another look at him, he exclaimed—

"Why it's Random! Good old Random; where on earth did he spring from?"

He patted the horse, and it was quite like the meeting of two friends after a long separation.

"I borrowed him," said Eli.

"From Mrs. Courtly?"

"Yes, and she was delighted to lend him."

"Will she be at the meet to-morrow?"

"No, only at the breakfast."

"I wonder what Warren will think when he sees me on him?" thought Ulick. "I expect she will merely explain that she lent him to Eli, and not mention my name."

He looked forward eagerly to riding his old favourite at a meet of the Rushshire hounds again, and yet he had strange misgivings when he was dressing, that something was about to happen which would change the whole course of his life. He had no inkling as to what it was, but the impression was there, and he could not get rid of it. He said nothing to Eli, and was as cheerful as usual at breakfast, and when he mounted Random he almost wished the day was over. He rode towards Helton, and met several people on horseback going to Hazelwell. Some of them recognised him, others he fancied did so but avoided looking in his direction.

James Bard, the veterinary surgeon, gave him a hearty welcome, and insisted on riding back with him to his house in the village.

"I am right glad to see you again," he said, briskly. "You have been away from us so long. I hope you have returned to stay."

"Not yet," replied Ulick. "I have not been to Hazelwell; I am going to join them as they pass through the village; they are sure to draw Brecon Wood first."

"Then I remain with you," said James Bard.

"You must go to Hazelwell; my father will miss you at the breakfast, and will be angry."

"Not when he learns why I remained away," replied Bard.

They rode together to James Bard's house, and remained there until the hounds came in sight. They stood at the window and watched them pass, and there was a large muster at the meet, the Hazelwell hunt breakfast always drawing a big crowd.

"It will be comparatively easy to remain unrecognised amongst that lot," said Ulick. "I did not see my father."

"The Squire has been down with the gout," said Bard, "and Dr. Harding has made him rest. I expect he will chafe a good deal at having to remain at home to-day."

Ulick was sorry his father had the gout, yet was glad he was absent from the hunt.

When the party cleared the village, James Bard and Ulick rode after them, in the direction of Brecon Wood.

As they neared the well-known haunt of the best foxes in Rushshire, they heard the hounds making music, and in a few minutes the well-known cry was heard, and they had "gone away" after the fox.

Ulick set Random going, and, followed by James Bard, quickly came in sight of the field. In front, well ahead, the hounds were streaming away over some open pastures, the fox going at a great pace, and the field in straggling order.

"He's got a capital start," said Ulick. "We are in for a good run."

"If it's the 'old dog' we went after last season, he'll make it hot. We shall soon tell, he generally doubles round and makes for Hazelwell Coppice at the other side of Glen church."

"Sixteen miles if it's a yard," said Ulick.

"And good going all the way, but there are some stiff fences, and we shall have to face the Tone river."

"Swim it or leap it?" laughed Ulick.

"You'll get over it on that fellow. I don't know about mine. I fancy I have seen yours before."

"So you have. It's Random."

"Good gracious, so it is. You'll have nothing to fear, and if anyone is in at the death, it will be yourself," said Bard.

It was not long before Random left the veterinary surgeon in the rear, and carried Ulick well to the front of the field. The horse fenced splendidly, and had a good rider on his back.

Warren Courtly inquired where Random was, and Irene told him she had lent him to Eli for a friend of his to ride, and with this he was satisfied, and did not ask who he was, much to her relief.

Ulick saw Warren ahead of him on a big Irish grey, a strong puller, but a good fencer, rather a dangerous horse to ride when his blood was up.

"He'll be surprised when he sees me on Random," thought Ulick, who had by this time forgotten all about his early-morning presentiment in the excitement of the chase.

They were galloping over a ploughed field, and the going was heavy, beyond was a meadow, and in the distance the river Tone could be seen. It was narrow in some parts, and not deep, but the banks were treacherous, and often brought riders to grief.

Out of the plough into the meadow they went at a fast pace. The old fox knew his way about, and bore away to the left. There was an old tree fallen, three parts of the way across the river, and he headed for it. Racing along the huge trunk with sure steps, he reached the end, made a long jump, and scrambled up the opposite side, and raced away up the steep incline towards Hazelwell Spinney and Glen church.

Warren set the grey at the water, and he cleared it gallantly. Ulick flew over on Random, and as they galloped up the hill got ahead of him, but was not within shouting distance as he passed him. At first Warren did not see him, but presently he recognised Random, and then Ulick.

He was never more surprised in his life than to see Ulick on Random at that particular moment. It staggered him for a few minutes, and when he recovered from the shock he was extremely angry.

"So it was to him she lent Random," he muttered savagely. "She knew he was here, at Helton. I wonder if they met when I was out. You shall suffer for this, Irene. Perhaps he thinks I am a coward; I'll show him who is the better man to-day. Damn him, I'll beat him, or know the reason why."

He rode the grey roughly, and the horse resented it. He pulled harder than ever, and the wild Irish blood in him revolted at his rider's handling.

Only half-a-dozen horsemen were near them, the bulk of the field had cut across country, knowing where the fox was making for. All the men following the track of the hounds were hard riders, and would have scorned to adopt such tactics.

"That's Ulick Maynard," muttered the huntsman. "I'm glad to see him out again, and on Random too. I wonder what he's done with old Eli's girl? She was a pretty wench. It was a bit rough on Eli, that was, and I didn't think Mr. Ulick was the man to do it. However, there's no telling what will happen when there's a woman in the case."

Ulick was thoroughly enjoying himself. He loved following the hounds, and had done so ever since he was a boy. He knew the country well, and was aware it would take Random all his time to keep going to the finish at this pace.

They were nearing Glen church, and beyond, in the distance,

was Hazelwell Coppice, the house being hidden amongst the trees a couple of miles away.

Ulick took in the well-remembered scene at a glance. He called to mind how he had galloped over this country with the Squire and Irene, and how they had found it a difficult task to keep up with his father. He wished Irene was there now, so that he could give her a lead over that big, stiff-set hedge a hundred yards ahead of him. He forgot all about Warren on the grey. There were the hounds scrambling through the bars of the gate, dashing through the holes in the hedge near the bank. Once he caught sight of the fox streaking along with his tail straight out, his head down, and his body almost level with the ground.

"He's not half done yet," thought Ulick. "He deserves to get away, and I hope he will save his brush."

The fox meant doing so if possible, there could be no doubt about that.

Round Glen church was a high, rough stone wall, built in the old style, stone piled upon stone, not bound together in any way, except by the pressure of one upon another. The coping on the top was loose, and in places big stones had rolled off on to the grass, for the church stood in a field, and was approached by a footpath.

The fox seemed of a pious turn of mind, for he headed straight for the church, as though hoping to find sanctuary there from his desperate pursuers.

Ulick expected to see him run round the churchyard, but instead of that he scrambled up the wall and made his way amongst the tombstones and over the graves of men who had hunted his ancestors in years gone by.

"If you think I am going to follow you over there you are mistaken," said Ulick. "I have no desire to join the silent residents in that locality. I'll ride round and catch you up on the other side, it is not far out of the way."

He watched the hounds scrambling over the rough wall, which stood on a rise on the ground, and saw from their movements they were well-nigh beaten.

Warren Courtly was not far behind. He saw Ulick check his

mount, and then make for the corner of the churchyard. He was near enough to be heard, if he shouted, and he called out—

"Follow me over the wall, if you have pluck enough; don't sneak round that way."

CHAPTER XIX

A FATAL LEAP

Ulick heard him, and, turning round, saw the grey galloping at a great pace straight for the churchyard wall. He did not accept the challenge; it would have been madness to do so. He called at the top of his voice to Warren to stop.

"He'll never clear it! Pull up!" shouted Ulick, excitedly.

For answer, Warren merely looked in his direction, and smiled grimly.

"Come on!" he shouted again. "Are you afraid?"

Ulick was not afraid, but he had no desire to break his neck, and that was probably what Warren would do if the grey failed to top the wall. There was no chance of stopping him, and Ulick determined to see the result of the dare-devil leap.

"He's mad to attempt it!" he said. "The horse is a good one, but he'll never get over it. I would not risk it on Random for a fortune!"

There was no one else near; the four or five horsemen had skirted round the wall, and were riding hard after the hounds, who had by this time cleared the churchyard.

Ulick waited for Warren's rash leap, and his heart almost stopped beating in his intense anxiety to see him safely over.

The presentiment of the morning flashed across his mind, and he wondered if this was to be the result.

Warren knew what lay before him; but his blood was up, and so was the grey's. The horse pricked his ears as he saw the formidable obstacle in front of him, but he did not shirk his work. On the contrary, he regulated his stride, and prepared for the desperate leap.

As Warren drew near to the wall Ulick rode forward, in order to render assistance should it be required, for he feared the result, and wished to do all in his power to help him.

Up the incline galloped the grey. Had the wall stood on the level he might have jumped it, although that was doubtful. The horse took off well, rose at the wall, and would have cleared it safely but for the fact that a huge raised gravestone, over a vault in the churchyard, stood close beneath it.

The horse saw it, tried to avoid it as he leaped, caught his hind legs on the wall, fell heavily forward, and threw Warren with terrific force head first on to the slab.

Ulick heard the crash and shuddered. Horse and rider failed to rise. He rode quickly to the spot, flung Random's bridle over a big coping stone, and scrambled over the wall, almost falling over the horse as he landed on the other side. He merely cast a rapid glance at the grey, and saw he was fatally injured, and rushed forward to Warren Courtly, who lay stretched out on the top of the slab where he had fallen.

Ulick stooped over him, and said, in an agitated voice—

"Warren! Warren! are you alive? Speak to me!"

There was no answer, no movement in the body, which lay dangerously still and inanimate.

Ulick tore open his vest and collar, and lifted him up. As he did so the head fell back, resting on his chest, and for a moment the eyes opened with the shock, but quickly closed again.

Ulick shuddered. That limp movement of the head, he knew what it meant. There was no hope. Warren's neck was broken. He had pitched on to his head, and the fall was bound to be fatal. He supported the dead man for a considerable time, hoping against hope that he would show some sign of life. His thoughts wandered to Irene, and he wondered how she would bear the shock. He must break it to her as gently as possible. She must hear it from no one but himself. He was of no use here. Warren was beyond human aid. He laid the body gently down, and covered the face with a handkerchief; it looked weird and uncanny, resting there in the scarlet coat on the top of a vault, in the picturesque old churchyard.

Getting over the wall, he remounted Random and rode away for assistance.

There was no one in sight. Then he espied two figures in the distance walking towards him; one was his father, the other Irene. They saw him, and his father waved his stick. There was no excuse; he had to pull up and meet them.

He was bewildered, at a loss what to do, what to say; and as he thought of Warren lying still in the churchyard he shuddered, and was almost tempted to make a bolt.

"You are not often out of the hunt," said the Squire. "Irene let the cat out of the bag, and told me you were here, and that Eli had borrowed Random for you. I am glad to see you out with the hounds again, but you ought to have come to breakfast."

"Have you had a fall, or missed the hounds?" asked Irene. "I am afraid I have taught Random bad manners. Have you seen Warren?"

He made no answer, but looked vacantly before him, and she said, anxiously, as she noticed the green moss from the stone on his coat—

"Have you hurt yourself? You look as though you have had a fall."

"I have not had a fall," he said, in a voice strangely unlike his own.

The Squire was quick at reading faces, and knew something had happened. Did it concern Irene? Had Warren been injured? He took her by the arm and said—

"Come, let us go home; and, as Ulick has missed the hounds, he can come with us."

Irene hesitated. She felt Ulick was concealing something, either from her or his father. What was it? Had anything happened to her husband?

She stepped forward before he dismounted, placing her hand on Random's neck, and, looking up into his face, said, quickly—

"Something has happened; I can see it in your face. There has been an accident. Is it Warren?"

He avoided her gaze. How could he tell her, and the churchyard where he lay quite close by?

The Squire saw there was serious news, and said, as cheerfully as possible—

"Has Warren had a spill? I hope it is not serious."

"Yes, he had a bad fall. I have just left him. I was riding for assistance when I met you."

Irene turned white, and the Squire supported her.

"Where is he?" she said. "Let me go to him."

Ulick dismounted and said—

"You must be brave, Irene! Warren has had a very bad fall."

"Where is he?" she asked again.

"He attempted to leap the churchyard wall and follow the hounds. It is a dangerous jump, and the horse fell, throwing him heavily."

"Then why do you delay? Ride for assistance at once! We will go to him," she said, and started off at a rapid pace in the direction of Glen church.

This was Ulick's opportunity. He stepped up to his father, and said—

"Do what you can to comfort her. He's in the churchyard, lying on Harewood's vault. I am better away."

"He is not——?" asked the Squire, and paused.

Ulick nodded. "He fell on his head on the slab and broke his neck. Now go after her."

"Call out to her to stop; I can hardly limp along," said the Squire.

"Irene!" called Ulick.

145

She turned round, and he pointed to his father.

She came hurriedly back, and said—

"Take my arm—we will go together."

Ulick mounted Random and rode rapidly away to Hazelwell, where he ordered a carriage and the requisite necessaries to be sent to the church, and dispatched a man for the doctor.

Meanwhile the Squire and Irene were nearing Glen church.

"Irene," he said, in a low voice, "Ulick has told me Warren is very badly injured; you must be prepared for the worst."

She looked at him with frightened eyes.

"Prepared for the worst!" she muttered. "Is his life in danger?"

"I am afraid so."

She gave a little sharp cry, and hurried forward again.

"You had better remain with me," he called, and she obeyed him without a murmur.

They reached the churchyard, and passed under the porch through the gateway, and at the far side, near the wall, the Squire saw a red coat on a tombstone; then he distinguished the form of a man. Irene had not seen it, and he led her down a side path.

"Be brave, Irene!" he said. "If he is in danger you will have to summon up all your courage to help him."

"I will," she said; "indeed I will."

Then she saw the red coat, and started back, her hand pressed against her heart, her eyes filled with horror.

"He is lying on the stone on the top of a vault," she said, in a hollow voice. "How did he get there?"

She stumbled forward over the graves, leaving the Squire to follow. She grazed her ankles, but heeded not, and at last she reached him.

Snatching the handkerchief away, she stood looking at his

146

face, with the closed eyes and the black mark on the neck. She stood perfectly still; no cry came from her; but her look of horror told she knew he was dead.

The Squire reached her just as she fell forward, insensible, on her husband's body. He lifted her tenderly in his arms, and sat down on the slab. With one hand he drew the handkerchief over Warren's face again.

"This is a sad blow," he thought. "It is a blessing she is insensible. It may be all for the best."

He allowed her to remain in this state for some minutes, and then tried to rouse her. His foot pained him, but he scarcely felt it.

Irene opened her eyes and shuddered. At first she did not realise where she was, but, as she caught sight of the gravestones, they recalled all.

"He is dead!" she said, slowly. "Poor Warren! he is dead!"

The tears came to her relief, and the Squire remained silent, with his arm supporting her.

Suddenly she flung herself on Warren's body and moaned bitterly.

The Squire placed his hand on her shoulder, and said—

"Irene, bear up; there is much to be done. We must take him home—to Hazelwell first, if you wish; it is nearer."

"No, no!" she said. "To the Manor. I want to be there with him alone!"

The carriage came, and was closely followed by Ulick and Dr. Harding, who examined Warren, and found his neck broken.

Tenderly they placed him in the carriage. Irene insisted upon getting in, and the Squire followed her, saying to Ulick—

"You and Dr. Harding had better follow us to the Manor."

Warren Courtly was taken back to his home, which he had left in the morning full of health and spirits, if not happiness. He little thought, when he mounted the fiery grey, how he was to return.

The news of the fatal accident soon spread, but it had not reached Anselm Manor, and there was consternation when they arrived.

Mrs. Dixon did all in her power for her mistress, and managed to calm and soothe her.

"It is dreadful!" moaned Irene.

She did not love Warren, but the shock of his death affected her terribly. It was so sudden, so unlooked for; and he was so young. She could hardly believe it. Dixon remained with her during the night, and towards early morning she sank into a troubled slumber.

"I cannot remain here," said Ulick, soon after their arrival. "It would not be right for me to do so. You will remain, father?"

"Yes; but you must go to Hazelwell," was the reply.

Warren was dead, and Irene knew nothing of his connection with Janet. He was glad of that; he had no hesitation in going to Hazelwell now.

"I will," he replied, and the Squire gave a sigh of relief.

"Home again, at last!" he thought. "Warren's death has brought us together again; once at Hazelwell he will not leave it."

Warren Courtly was buried in Anselm church, in the vault where several of his ancestors reposed; and Irene was a widow, having been only a very short time a wife, and that only in name.

It was a shock to the county, and the members of the Rushshire Hunt in particular, and it was generally acknowledged Warren's rashness at attempting such a leap caused his early death.

Ulick and the Squire examined the wall where the grey and his rider were killed, and the latter said—

"I wonder what made him attempt it? As a rule he was not rash."

Ulick explained what had happened, and how Warren had dared him to follow him.

"I wonder sometimes if he was angry because Irene lent me Random to ride, and that caused him to act as he did."

"I should not be disposed to look at it in that light," answered his father. "He may have been surprised to see you out, more especially on Random; but there was no harm in your riding him. There was something else at the bottom of the challenge he threw out to you. Did you ever doubt his courage?"

"If I did, he was unaware of it," was the answer.

"Then it must have been in a sudden fit of rashness he did it," said the Squire.

Janet Todd read the account of the fatal accident to Warren Courtly in the paper, but she did not grieve much over his death, although she felt sorry it had taken place. There was nothing now to hinder her returning to her father, and it was the only thing she could do, as she had very little money.

She wrote to Eli begging his forgiveness, and asking if he would take her back. Needless to say, his reply was loving and fatherly, and he implored her to come home without delay.

Janet returned, and Eli—good, large-hearted man that he was—received her with open arms, and she was grateful for his kindness.

Some weeks after her return he said to her one night—

"Janet, I had made up my mind never to allude to the past, but I will ask you one question and have done with it."

She knew what the question was, and decided there could be no harm in answering it now, more especially as Irene knew the whole circumstances.

"I will answer any question you care to ask me," she said.

"Who induced you to run away and leave me?" he asked.

"Warren Courtly."

"I thought as much," was his reply.

CHAPTER XX

PERFECT HARMONY

It was over twelve months since Warren Courtly came to an untimely end, and the Squire and his son were in the morning-room, where he had kept vigil on the anniversary of Ulick's departure. There was no snow on this occasion, as they looked out of the window at the familiar scene; but the ground was held in the grip of a hard frost, and the white crystals had not yet vanished from the trees.

"Irene is coming for dinner to-night," said the Squire, as he looked at him.

"And who else is coming?"

"Only Dr. Harding and the Vicar and his wife," replied his father.

Ulick did not immediately reply, but stood at the window while the Squire sat down.

Bersak, who was lying on the hearthrug, went to him and licked his hand. He patted the dog's head, but, as he made no movement to go away, Bersak went and laid down at the Squire's feet.

During the months that had elapsed since Warren's death he had seen very little of Irene, had, in fact, avoided her as much as possible, and absented himself a good deal from Hazelwell, his excuse being that he liked to see his horses run, especially the Saint.

The "curiosity" had won some good handicaps, and, at the Squire's request, he had been sent down to Hazelwell at the end of his four-year-old career, much to Fred May's chagrin, as he wished to keep him in work, and said it was throwing money away to send him to the stud at that age. Ulick, however, wished to please his father, so the Saint was now an important member of the Hazelwell stud, and Eli Todd was as proud of him as the trainer had been.

The Squire knew it was not altogether racing that caused his son to vanish from home for weeks at a time. He appreciated the delicacy of feeling which actuated him and took him away from Irene's presence in the early months of her widowhood. He saw in his conduct a sure sign that he was in love with her, and he gleaned from Irene's look of disappointment, when she saw Ulick was absent, that she returned his affection.

It had always been a thorn in the Squire's side that he had induced Irene to marry Warren Courtly, who was unsuited to her, and had thus placed an insurmountable barrier in Ulick's way.

By an accident that obstacle had been removed, and he did not intend his cherished idea should again come to nothing.

The Squire did not mourn for Warren Courtly. He was no hypocrite, and, although sorry for his early death, he argued that it was all for the best, more especially when he came to examine into his affairs, and afterwards when he had made Janet tell him who had run away with her. This she did on giving his word he would keep her secret.

Warren, who had left the Squire joint executor with Irene, had involved the Anselm estate heavily, and it would take some years to wipe off the debt that had accumulated. Irene had a considerable income, but not more than half she had a right to have expected. There was a mortgage on the Manor itself, but the Squire quickly took that up on his own account.

As Ulick looked out of the window, his thoughts were busy with memories of the past, and in them Irene was a conspicuous figure. He had waited more than twelve months, and held his peace, although he was impatient to pour out his love to her now she was free. He was thinking whether he would have an opportunity of doing so to-night, and, if it occurred, whether he would take it. What would her answer be? He did not wish to be over-confident, but he looked forward to a favourable reply, and his heart beat fast in expectation.

He was not aware Irene knew who ran away with Janet, and he was pleased to think she had no knowledge of Warren's conduct.

His father watched him with a smile on his face, and thought—

"He means to ask her to-night. He is making up his mind, and I will see he has the chance."

"Is there anything particularly striking to look at out there?" asked the Squire. "If so, I will join you."

Ulick laughed as he replied, "I was taking very little notice of the view. I was thinking over old times."

"Pleasant thoughts?"

"Yes, most of them."

"We were a couple of fools to remain separated for such a long time," said the Squire.

"We appreciate being together again the more now," replied Ulick.

"Eli is precious glad to have that girl of his back again," said the Squire. "I hope the lesson she has had will teach her to behave better in the future."

"There is no fear about that," replied Ulick. "It has been severe."

"Not nearly so severe as she deserved," was the reply.

It was a merry dinner party, and they were all in high spirits. Later on in the evening the Squire and the Vicar's wife challenged the Vicar and the Doctor to a quiet rubber, which was eagerly accepted.

"You two young people can look after yourselves," said the Squire to Irene and his son, and she flushed slightly at his words.

Whist was an interesting game to the players, but Ulick and Irene evidently found it slow as spectators, and quietly left the room.

A bright fire was blazing in the drawing-room, and Irene sat down at the piano and idly ran her hands over the keys. The lamps shed a soft, yellow light over the room, and the effect was soothing and tranquil.

Presently Irene sang a simple song, and, when it was ended, went on with another. She was fond of music; so was Ulick, and he listened to her sweet, low notes, and watched her face as she sang, half unconscious of his presence.

When she stopped and looked up she found him standing near her. Their eyes met, and, taking her hand, he said—

"Irene, I have something to say to you."

She knew what he meant, and knew what her answer must be.

He pleaded his cause well, and she listened, smiling encouragement when he faltered.

He asked her to be his wife, and she consented without any false hesitation.

They were very happy, and Ulick felt that somehow the world was a very good place to live in, and that the ways of life were not quite so crooked as some people were desirous of making out.

He could not realise that Irene had ever been Warren Courtly's wife. He seemed to have possessed her ever since she came to Hazelwell on the death of her father. She was his Irene, always had been, and always would be for ever more.

And Irene was very happy. She knew her brief life with Warren had been all a mistake. She regretted his death, and the manner of it, but it had not blighted her life. She had known of people who had mourned distractedly the loss of a dear one, and in a few months had changed the garments of widowhood for those of marriage.

In a few years Warren would be merely a memory, nothing more, and it had been his own fault. Having neglected her during life, it was not reasonable to expect he would be reverenced when dead.

She knew she had always loved Ulick, although she had been unaware of it, and now the realisation of her happiness was at hand.

She was to remain at Hazelwell for the night, and when the other guests departed the Squire was told what had happened.

"I knew it was coming," he said, joyfully. "I saw it in your faces. Come and kiss me, Irene; you are not jealous, are you, Ulick?"

"Not at all," he replied, laughing; "but I envy you."

"What!" he exclaimed. "Not had one yet?"

"Dozens," whispered Irene, in his ear, and the Squire laughed heartily.

"You recollect this room when I sat up all night waiting for Ulick to return?" said the Squire.

"Yes," replied Irene; and then she added, "it is the very day."

"So it is, my child," he replied, "and I take it as a happy omen for your married life."

In the summer, when the trees were full of leaf, and the birds carolled their sweetest and best, Ulick and Irene were married. It was a quiet wedding, and they went abroad for some considerable time. On their return they resided at Anselm Manor, and the Squire divided his time between Hazelwell and their home.

Ulick had learned from his wife that she knew all about Janet and Warren, and it was not long before they found out that the Squire was in possession of the facts. As for Janet, she accepted the position of lady's maid to Irene when Mary Marley and Bob Heather were married. This bold move on Irene's part effectually silenced the gossips, who clung to the belief that Ulick was the cause of Janet's trouble, and that they had run away together. It was acknowledged that Mrs. Maynard would never have had Janet in her service had such been the case.

Happiness reigned supreme at Anselm Manor, and when the Squire heard of the arrival of a son, and that he was a grandfather, he gave a whoop of joy that startled the decorous quietude of Hazelwell.

"And if it isn't on the very day, the same day that Ulick left me, and the day on which Irene consented to be his wife."

The new arrival made the Squire feel young again, and no signs were wanting that the little one would be a prime favourite with him.

Years soon roll by and time never stands still. The child grew into a fine boy, and there were others to keep him company. There was every sign that Anselm Manor would be the home of many happy children. The laughter of youth rang through the old rooms, and echoed down the passages and along the walls, where monks and friars had revelled and prayed and told their beads hundreds of years before. Anselm Manor had taken on a new lease of life; a new spirit was infused into it—the buoyant spirit of youth.

Ulick and his wife were often seen in the hunting field, and occasionally at some of the principal race meetings; and there was much rejoicing at Hazelwell when Fred May pulled off the Jockey Club Stakes with the colt out of Honeysuckle, that had only just escaped being born nearly "a year old."

The Saint was making a name at the stud, and his early foals were promising, but none of them were the colour of their sire.

Ulick, however, wanted a grey by him, and in due time got his wish, and a promising youngster he looked.

Janet did not forget Mrs. Hoffman. The woman had been kind to her in her way, and she often received a present from the Manor. As for Felix Hoffman, he got into trouble with the police, and had to leave the country in a hurry, only just escaping the meshes of the law, in which he thoroughly deserved to be entangled.

Squire Maynard, so everyone said, had grown young since his son's marriage with Irene, and a fine, noble country gentleman he looked as he walked or rode, with his grandson on a cob at his side.

Young Ulick was very like the Squire, who saw his own youth reflected in him, and indulged him accordingly.

Irene, as a mother, was far more attractive than she had ever been before, and her husband and children adored her. They were proud of her good looks and of the admiration she invariably excited.

Ulick sometimes thought of that fatal leap Warren Courtly took when he passed Glen church, and saw again the red-coated figure on the cold slab near the wall, but the melancholy remembrance quickly vanished. There is too much sunshine in his life to be hidden by passing clouds, and happiness leaves no room for discord. Everything is in harmony; there are no jarring notes; and long may it be so with them all.

THE END